## Aidan had to show Frankie this engagement ploy was a mistake.

"Are you prepared to be my fiancé?" she asked.

"Of course," he replied automatically. "I always go the distance in my investigations."

"And in other areas?"

"Are you flirting with me?"

She closed the distance and pressed her lips to his. Warmth spread from that point of contact down his arms, sizzling in his fingertips as her gaze held him captive. Then her eyelids drifted shut. She pushed her hand into his hair and drew him closer for a full, sensual kiss that blasted through him like a flash grenade.

She was like a double shot of whiskey with a drop of honey—all fire with a hint of sweetness. He changed the angle, tipping up her chin and taking control of the kiss. When her lips parted on a sigh, he slid his tongue across hers with bold strokes.

"I think that will convince anyone," she said.

It sure as hell convinced him.

# GUNNING FOR THE GROOM

USA TODAY Bestselling Authors

## DEBRA WEBB & REGAN BLACK

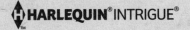

HARLEQUIN® INTRIGUE®

With many thanks to Kim, for your wealth of patience,
love and priceless friendship!

Recycling programs
for this product may
not exist in your area.

ISBN-13: 978-0-373-74946-1

Gunning for the Groom

**HARLEQUIN**®

™ www.Harlequin.com

**Printed in U.S.A.**

**Debra Webb**, born in Alabama, wrote her first story at age nine and her first romance at thirteen. It wasn't until she spent three years working for the military behind the Iron Curtain—and a five-year stint with NASA—that she realized her true calling. Since then the *USA TODAY* bestselling author has penned more than one hundred novels, including her internationally bestselling Colby Agency series.

**Regan Black**, a *USA TODAY* bestselling author, writes award-winning, action-packed novels featuring kick-butt heroines and the sexy heroes who fall in love with them. Raised in the Midwest and California, she and her family, along with their adopted greyhound, two arrogant cats and a quirky finch, reside in the South Carolina Lowcountry, where the rich blend of legend, romance and history fuels her imagination.

### Books by Debra Webb and Regan Black

### Harlequin Intrigue

### *Colby Agency: Family Secrets*

*Gunning for the Groom*

### *The Specialists: Heroes Next Door*

*The Hunk Next Door*
*Heart of a Hero*
*To Honor and To Protect*
*Her Undercover Defender*

Visit the Author Profile page at
Harlequin.com for more titles.

# CAST OF CHARACTERS

*Francesca (Frankie) Leone*—The daughter of an army general, Frankie served as a cultural liaison with a navy SEAL team until an injury forced her to retire. Now she's searching for the truth behind the tragic accusations that led her father to commit suicide.

*Aidan Abbot*—Formerly with Interpol, Aidan was added to Victoria Colby-Camp's team of expert investigators based in the Chicago office. He's tasked with protecting Frankie as she follows a new lead.

*Sophia Leone*—Frankie's mother, a recent widow, and also the co-owner of Leo Solutions, a security company she and her husband once dreamed of establishing after he retired.

*Paul Sterling*—Sophia's business partner in Leo Solutions, his focus is growth of the company as well as his relationship with Sophia.

*Victoria Colby-Camp*—The semiretired head of the Colby Agency. She and her husband, Lucas Camp, can't seem to stay out of the business of investigations.

# Chapter One

*Chicago, Illinois*
*Wednesday, April 6, 5:30 p.m.*

Victoria Colby-Camp rose from her desk and turned to her beloved window. She watched the gentle spring rain falling upon the city she would always call home. Evening lights twinkled, reminding her that it was time to go home. *Home.* A smile tugged at her lips. How had she considered for even a moment that any other city on earth could take the place of Chicago?

The most wonderful years of her life, as well as the most painful ones, had played out here. Her son was here, as were her beautiful grandchildren. No matter how warm it was or how much sun south Texas had to offer, it would never be the Windy City.

Sensing Lucas's presence, she turned, her smile widening automatically. She had loved this man for so very long. Even when her first husband, James Colby, was alive, Lucas Camp had been her dearest friend. The two of them waited many years before allowing that lifelong bond to bloom into a more intimate relationship. Their wedding day had been one of the happiest of her life—in part because that momentous occasion came almost at the same time that her son found his way back to her. Jim Colby had been missing for twenty years when he came back into her life. So many miracles had happened that year.

Victoria's life had come full circle now. Her family was safe and happy and she was back in the city she loved.

"You're ready to go?" she asked, when Lucas remained in the doorway.

"No hurry. I could stand here forever just looking at you."

"Lucas, you're too kind." Even after all these years as man and wife, she could feel her pulse react to his voice, as well as the compliment. "I'm ready."

Tomorrow was another day at the Colby Agency offices and she couldn't wait to see what it held.

# Chapter Two

"Morning, Frankie!"

Francesca Leone, Frankie to everyone who knew her longer than a few minutes, smiled on her way to the office she shared with two other people. It wasn't much more than a converted storage space, but she didn't mind. She'd worked in tighter quarters during her time with the navy. Life in Georgia had been good to her. Landing this job as an analyst with the Savannah Police Department gave her a healthy, long overdue sense of renewed purpose.

The past eighteen months had been an arduous journey personally and professionally. An act of terrorism and the resulting injury had ended the navy career she'd loved. For too many months, her life had narrowed to a pinpoint focus on surviving the physical trials, only to be assaulted by the emotional upheaval that followed. She hadn't realized how much of her identity had been tied to her military service until it was gone. But here she'd found a fresh start and was building a strong new foundation, far from the looming shadow of her father's name and the constant worried gaze of her mother.

Feeling her back aching a bit from yesterday's extended run, she eased into the desk chair, setting her mug of tea to the left of her computer monitor and locking her purse in the bottom drawer. When her computer booted up, she wasted no time getting to work. A string of recent robberies crossed several precincts, and it was her job to find any connections to help the detectives create a list of suspect traits.

Although the work didn't rank as high in the elements of danger and thrill as her former SEAL team missions, she found tremendous fulfillment when her contributions helped close cases.

She was making notes on the similarities between thefts when her desk phone rang, and she picked it up. "Leone."

"Francesca Leone?"

She didn't recognize the quiet male voice on the other end of the line. "Yes." Pausing to glance around when someone called her by her proper name was a purely instinctive reaction. "How can I help you?"

"I worked with your dad on several operations," the man explained.

Her heart stuttered in her chest. It never seemed to beat properly when the topic of her dad came up. She bit her lip, refusing to deliver the coarse response on the tip of her tongue.

"I considered him a friend," the caller said into the prolonged silence.

And yet she noticed he didn't offer her a name. She wasn't an idiot. Since her father, General Frank Leone, had been accused and convicted of treason, no one claimed any kind of link to him. This couldn't be an old friend who'd lost touch or wanted to leave the general's daughter with a memorable photo.

Smelling a setup, she decided the caller must be a reporter sniffing out a new story angle. Unfortunately for him, there weren't any. It had been over a year since the verdict, and her review of every available shred of information had yet to yield any solid intel that could remove the terrible stain on her dad's career. "What do you want?"

"First, I'm sorry for your loss."

Her hand fisted around the receiver, but she didn't take the bait. Her father had killed himself ten months ago, shortly after the verdict came down. While she wasn't over it, she never let that weakness show—to strangers or friends.

"I just need a few minutes of your time," the caller said. "Your father trusted me with something you should have."

Curious now, she checked the urge to slam down the phone. "All right." A face-to-face chat was the fastest way to determine if there was anything legitimate about this guy. "And your name?"

"When we meet," he replied.

She'd anticipated that response. Odds were he wouldn't have given her a real name, anyway. "How will I know you?"

"I'll know *you.*"

Of course he would. Growing up on various army bases around the world with two parents who rated the highest possible security clearances, Frankie valued caution and understood paranoia. "Fine. Meet me at Bess's Diner in the historic district in an hour." That would give her plenty of time to drive by and get her head on straight.

Fifty minutes later she sat in her car, studying a man leaning against a bike rack in front of the diner across the street. Short, graying brown hair; late forties, early fifties maybe. Assuming he was the caller, she was pleased he didn't give off the hum of urgency she'd learned to expect from reporters. While nothing about him struck her as familiar, in her experience the best covert agents were comfortable hiding in plain sight. As she climbed out of her car, she inconspicuously snapped a couple of pictures with her phone. If the man really knew her dad, he'd know about her mother's work, and her own abbreviated career, as well.

Or maybe this wasn't the guy at all, she thought when he didn't react as she crossed to his side of the street. She didn't acknowledge him as she aimed for the diner door.

"Miss Leone." His voice proved she had a few instincts left. "Thanks for following through."

"Sure." She stopped, kept her stance easy and her hands loose at her sides while she waited for him to make the next move.

"Name's John," he said, extending a hand. "Your father was a good friend of mine."

John. She nearly asked if the last name was Smith or Doe. Not that it mattered. Anyone openly admitting to being General Leone's friend had bigger secrets than a name. She suddenly wished she had something more to go on than his pictures in case she needed to track him down after this meeting. His was one of those nondescript faces that would be hard to remember. This close, she could see that his eyes were brown, as well. Straight nose. No scars. The kind of face that would blend in with the crowd.

They walked into the diner and found a booth. She noticed he took the side facing the door. If this guy didn't have covert operations training, he'd read all the right books. When the waitress approached, John ordered coffee and Frankie ordered hot tea with honey. She wasn't in the mood for anything, just wanted something to keep her hands busy while she listened to whatever John had to say.

"Your dad and I go way back," he said. "I count Frank and Sophia as my closest friends."

Frankie couldn't hide the unpleasant chill she felt at the mention of her mother's name. She hadn't spoken to the woman since her father's funeral. The once proud and strong Leone family had been fractured beyond any hope of reconciliation.

"You still on the outs with her?"

"Why does it matter?" Keeping things compartmentalized was practically a Leone genetic trait. Frankie's personal life didn't intersect with her professional life. She never discussed her parents with anyone. Clearly, this man knew the family dynamic, though the situation was fairly obvious. Her mother lived and worked in Seattle, while Frankie lived and worked here, as far away as possible. She still periodically checked for jobs in Key West, Florida. There were questions she knew she'd never get answered, so Frankie clung to the simple truth that distance preserved the peace.

"It doesn't." John leaned back as the coffee and tea arrived. When the waitress walked away, he continued. "Look, I know you were close to him and I know he was proud of your career."

"Thanks?" His well-informed statements didn't put her at ease. They only made her more uncomfortable. She stirred a spoonful of honey into her tea and went on the offensive, eager to hurry this along. "Any decent search of the internet could give you that much," she said. "When I was first attached to the SEAL team, they did a write-up in the local paper, got a glowing quote from him." She set the spoon aside. "Tell me why we're here."

The man's brown eyes were sharp as he studied her. "Because your father was a hero and someone turned him into a scapegoat."

Whatever his real name, she agreed with John on that much. Her biggest regret was that she hadn't been there for her dad during the ordeal. Injured or not, she resented that she'd never had a chance to tell him she believed he was innocent, or that she loved him despite the stones thrown from all sides. There hadn't been any tender farewell phone call or last words in a note. When her father made a decision, he followed through. He'd killed himself shortly after the guilty verdict, before she'd regained her ability to walk unassisted.

The memories of hearing the news swamped her and she raised her tea to her lips, the cup shaking slightly. Sophia, with no trace of emotion, had explained her husband's suicide and told Frankie what would come next regarding services, the will and estate, and the rest of it. In the days immediately following the tragedy, Frankie had tried to talk to her, hoping to make sense of the senseless. Her mother had been too wrapped up in the legalities and had quickly moved on as though a lifetime of marriage and family had meant nothing.

"He'd be happy to see you strong and healthy again."

John's quiet voice brought Frankie back to the present with an unpleasant jolt.

"I like to think so." She carefully placed the cup in the saucer.

"You've done well reestablishing yourself."

"Uh-huh." She toyed with the handle of her cup. "You said you had something for me?" She didn't want to talk about her father or her new life. Not with a therapist, not with a friend, and definitely not with a stranger.

"Yes." He reached into the pocket inside his sport coat and fished out a small gray envelope. "This matches a safe-deposit box in Tucson," he explained, his voice no more than a whisper. With one finger he pushed the envelope, which presumably held a key, halfway across the table. "No one mattered to your dad as much as you did. He can't tell you in his own words, but the answers you're after are there."

*Answers.* Frankie blinked away the rush of tears blurring her vision. She'd expected dog tags, or maybe her dad's class ring from West Point. Answers were a thousand times better. She hadn't been prepared for someone who believed her father had been railroaded, and wanted to help her ferret out the truth. She caught her trembling lower lip between her teeth and fought valiantly for composure. There would be time for emotions later. "How do you know what answers I'm after?" she asked, using his phrase. "Dad's case is closed." It was hard to believe this could be the break she needed to clear her father's name.

John left the envelope on the table, pulling his fingers back and drumming them on the rim of his coffee cup, watching her closely. "The case is officially closed, but it's nowhere near done for you. You take that and you'll have a chance to right a wrong."

She couldn't tear her eyes away from that slim gray envelope. "Why don't *you* do what's necessary with the information?"

He shook his head. "This is for family. I'm just the messenger."

Frankie sucked in a breath. He couldn't mean what those words implied. She'd learned that her mother's testimony had come into play during her father's trial, though Frankie had never understood why it hadn't helped. Sophia refused to discuss the matter, which left Frankie with more questions than answers at every turn.

"From where I'm sitting I'd say you got that stubbornness and tenacity from your dad," John said, urging her on in his quiet way.

Frankie covered the envelope with her hand, pulling it closer to her side of the table. Either she hadn't been as discreet as she should have been or John had the depth of access that went with the cloak-and-dagger routine. She thought of the inquiries she'd made after her father's funeral. All of them had turned into frustrating dead ends. Hope surged through her that this key would unlock the secrets about General Leone's final missions overseas.

She peered into the envelope before tucking it into her pocket. Taking it didn't mean she had to do anything about it. She studied John's inscrutable face. "How can I reach you?"

"You can't." His gaze moved systematically around the coffee shop. "My being here, even for a few hours, puts you in jeopardy. This has to be our only communication."

She gave a short nod as her mind reeled. This man was the first person who showed any sign of agreeing with her about her father's innocence.

John pulled out his wallet and tossed a ten-dollar bill onto the table. "You don't have to go and you don't have to be in a hurry," he said. "In fact, I recommend you take some time and think it through. What's inside the box isn't going anywhere."

She knew she had to go. She couldn't ignore this opportunity. A flight to Arizona was nothing in the bigger picture. Her family had imploded under the treason accusation. Knowing her father had died disgraced and alone, Frankie still felt an ache in her heart. If there was any information that would cast a light of truth into those dark final days and clear his name, she meant to find it. "I'll go." As soon as she could arrange a few days off work.

Getting to Tucson was the easy part of the equation. There was no way to tell what would come next until she'd seen the contents of the box for herself. After the last lead dried up a few months ago, she'd been less aggressive in her private inquiry, resigned that she might never learn who'd set up her dad. Cautiously pushing hope aside, she considered that this meeting and the trip to open a safe-deposit box could be nothing more than an elaborate ruse or distraction, though she didn't know who would gain by such a tactic.

"What you discover could make things worse," John warned.

"Thanks," she whispered, stunned by the dramatic shift her morning had taken. The key in its envelope felt like a stick of old dynamite in her pocket, shaky, volatile and ready to blow her life apart without any notice. "Unless you have more insight, I guess I'll figure that out when I get there."

"Whatever you decide, be careful." He slid to the edge of the booth. "The people who took down your dad have a long reach and violent habits."

She resisted the urge to try to enlist his help. He'd clearly done all he was going to do. "I can take care of myself." She'd trained hard to earn her place as a cultural liaison with the navy SEALs. Her well-honed skills and habit of excellence hadn't been affected by the back injury that wrecked her military career.

"I hope so." He stood up. "Your dad always wanted the best for you."

Frankie believed that was true. She watched her father's mysterious friend leave, disappointed when he walked out of view. She'd hoped to catch him getting into a car. Staring into the tea cooling in her cup, she weighed the pros and cons of each possible next step. Did the cons even matter? Every decision in life came with a price; every option held some risk.

Her gaze shifted to the window and the bustling activity on the street outside. She had a new career as a crime analyst. She enjoyed it. Her life was stable and she gained satisfaction in the work and being involved with the community. And she knew herself well enough to know that part of her fulfillment came from finding justice for victims.

The whole truth wouldn't bring her father back, but it could open the door for justice and potentially restore his reputation. He'd served honorably and deserved to be remembered for the way he'd protected national interests, as well as the soldiers under his command.

She pulled out her phone and researched flight options. By the time she got back to the office, she had her explanation ready and a realistic idea of the days off she would need to run down this lead.

*Tucson, Arizona*
*Friday, April 8, 8:40 a.m.*

FRANKIE CHECKED OUT of her hotel room and left the cool lobby for the warm sunshine of the Arizona springtime. Her boss had waved away her vague explanation of a family crisis and granted her time off through the end of next week. It helped that Frankie could do much of her work long-distance if necessary. She'd gotten on a plane last night. Waiting for morning had proved one of the hardest things she'd done in a while.

Hailing a cab, she gave the driver the bank address as her mind raced yet another lap around the same tired circuit that had plagued her since she left the diner yesterday. Every time she reviewed what she'd learned since her father's death, the timing of the charges and the sequence of events, she bumped smack into her mother's uncharacteristic behavior and apathy. Her mom was hiding something; Frankie just couldn't guess what or why. Hopefully, whatever her father had stashed in this safe-deposit box would take her a step closer to the truth.

Sophia, as a military analyst for the CIA, had the clearance access and professional connections to support the general's defense. At the very least, she should've given Frankie a better explanation for how things had spiraled out of control. Her injury and recovery weren't a reliable excuse any longer. Neither was the nonsense about Frankie's career being negatively impacted by her father's misdeeds.

He was *innocent*. Whatever had happened during those last few months in Afghanistan, Frankie knew her father hadn't betrayed his oath to his country, and she meant to prove it.

It was a relief when the cab stopped and she had to think about paying the fare. Taking her suitcase and the backpack serving as her laptop bag and purse, she headed inside the bank, then paused to look around. She didn't know why her dad had chosen this facility. They'd never lived on the nearby post, though she was sure both her parents had been here at one time or another, since Fort Huachuca was home to the Army Intelligence Center.

Frankie offered a polite smile as she showed her key and requested access to the safe-deposit box. Her palms were damp as she followed the teller toward the vault, the wheels of her suitcase rattling over the marble floor. When both keys had been inserted into the respective locks, the teller pulled out the slim drawer and walked toward a small alcove.

"Just draw the curtain back when you're done," she said. "And we'll replace the box for you."

"Got it. Thanks," Frankie said as the woman walked away.

She stared at the closed safe-deposit box on the table, her feet rooted in place. Now she had second thoughts. Her dad had left her something here, something he hadn't trusted to her mom's care. The truth of her father's downfall could very well be inside. Frankie had come this far; she had to see it through. One step, then another, and she rested her trembling fingers on the cool metal box. John's warning echoed in her head. She believed with every beat of her heart that her father had been a scapegoat. Whoever had gone to those lengths to avoid the consequences obviously didn't want to be exposed.

If she looked inside, there would be no going back, no way to undo whatever she learned. Holding back or walking away—those weren't valid options, either. Not for Frankie.

"Don't have to like it, just have to do it." She whispered one of the favorite motivators from her SEAL training as she opened the box. She didn't have to act on it; she just had to know.

An envelope marked Top Secret was no surprise, though surely the evidence against her father should rate a higher clearance level. Under the envelope she found a flash drive, half a map and two passports. Slipping the drive into her pocket, she discovered both passports had her mother's picture beside different names and birth dates.

Assuming John had gathered the evidence in this box on her father's behalf, Frankie wondered how he'd gotten the passports away from her mom. Seduction or burglary? A small voice in her head suggested this field trip was a setup, and Frankie's temper flared in bitter denial. John was a wild card, definitely, but she would not leap to any conclusions until she'd exhausted every lead.

Frankie tamped down her frustration. The attention an outburst would bring was the last thing she needed here. She tucked the fake passports into her backpack and kept going.

A smaller envelope held her father's dog tags, and her heart stuttered in her chest. She looped the cool metal chain around her fingers. When she was little, her dad had often let her wear his tags when she played dress up with his boots and uniforms. If she'd had any doubts about John's claims, the dog tags dispelled them. With care, she poured the tags and chain back into the envelope and added it to her backpack. Only one item remained, a small jewelry box covered in worn black velvet.

Her fingers curled back into her palm. That box didn't belong here. Her father had kept it on top of his dresser in the bedroom. The ring inside came out only for official functions.

Frankie popped open the lid, praying she was wrong, that this was something else. It wasn't. She bit her lip, staring down at her father's class ring from West Point. Snapping the box shut, she pressed it close to her heart, as if somehow that would make everything that had gone wrong right again.

This ring was central to her image of her dad, of the honor, dedication and commitment he'd given to every endeavor. She opened the box again, smoothing her finger over the heavy gold band. All her life she'd watched him, captivated by the stories he told as he polished it for special occasions. She'd caught him once just holding it, dazed, when he returned from a deployment. Her mother had told her later that one of his classmates had died.

When had he stored it here and why? Frankie couldn't think of a single answer to either question. "I'll figure it out, Dad. I promise," she murmured, sliding the ring box into a zippered inner pocket of the backpack.

Finally, she unwound the red string tying the large envelope closed and shook out the papers inside. After-action reports were on top. She skimmed each page, noting the details that weren't blacked out. The dates and locations matched what she already knew of General Leone's final months in Afghanistan.

She forgot everything else when she found the transcript of her mother's statement about his activities in Afghanistan. Icy dread tickled the nape of Frankie's neck and she steeled herself against the involuntary shiver. Sophia Leone had created a report that didn't support her husband at all. She'd tossed him under the proverbial bus.

What the hell? Her parents had *always* been a team. From Frankie's first memory they'd been affectionate and happy, devoted to each other. They'd embraced life, taught her everything she valued about being in love and being loving. They'd exemplified respect, support and drive as they went after their individual and mutual goals together.

How could Sophia turn on him?

Frankie blinked back a red haze of fury as she read the cold, sterile statements that tied her father to criminal actions. Fumed over the *implications* that he'd sabotaged missions for personal gain. The report did nothing to corroborate General Leone's account of critical operations. Good grief, in light of this statement, no other verdict than guilty had been possible.

Frankie pulled out the band holding her hair in a bun and worked her fingers over her scalp.

At least she understood why her mother had refused to discuss any of this. Frankie wound her hair back up into place as she read the terrible statement again.

Two dates stood out to her, dates when she knew her father had been at the Bagram Airfield, when her mother stated he'd been in Kabul. She checked her watch, wishing she had time to boot up her computer and check the flash drive here. Now that she had a lead, she was eager to chase it down. With any luck the drive would have more details she could assess and pull into a cohesive case against her mother. No wonder her dad had killed himself. Someone had set him up so well with the treason charge that even his wife had turned on him.

"And I was useless," Frankie whispered to herself. During his trial she'd been stuck in a hospital bed while surgeons debated the best treatment for her spine injury.

She fisted the papers in her hands as something inside her shattered. John had warned her and he'd been right. Appalling as this was, the answers gave her a target. Sophia owed her more than another weak evasion. Frankie had asked her mother point-blank about the allegations and charges against her dad, and the answer had been to trust the legal process and keep believing in him.

Frankie had obediently complied and the process had failed her father. Along with a helpful boost from her mother, apparently. Even after the verdict, her mom had insisted things would work out, that her father wasn't done fighting. Now it was obvious those assurances had merely been more lies and platitudes to cover Sophia's part in the witch hunt.

Why? Who gained? Her mother had put the life insurance and other assets into a trust for Frankie, and turned her attention to a new private security business out in Seattle, Washington.

After stuffing the papers back into the envelope, Frankie secured the tie, suddenly uncertain. Was it safer to leave the evidence here or take it with her?

John had given her one key. Typically, safe-deposit boxes were issued with two. He'd told her that his visit, brief and cryptic as it was, put her at risk. She hadn't done anything to hide her travel plans, so if someone were watching, whoever it was could easily conclude she'd been here. She decided to take everything and create a new hiding place.

John must have gathered the legal and personal items on her dad's orders. Frank would've known his daughter would never buy in to the treason charges. He wanted her to clear his name—Frankie felt it like a flame deep in her heart. If he believed in her to do that, why kill himself?

Confused and hurt, she couldn't quite see the next step beyond leaving Arizona. Her gut instinct was to fly out to Seattle and confront her mother. Just the thought had Frankie braced for a battle. Showing up in a fit of anger wouldn't help. Her mom was far too composed, too deft at sliding around the truth for a direct attack.

There was no way Frankie could do this until she calmed down, planned it out. She needed to go through the flash drive and it would be smart to get a second opinion on the documents, just in case John was playing her.

She thought about the dog tags and the West Point ring as she rubbed her knuckles across the scars and tight muscles at her back. If that was the case, she had to give him points for knowing his target.

"Think, Frankie." There were always options. Her military training had changed her way of thinking. As a SEAL she'd embraced the clever and creative strategies required for a small force to succeed when outnumbered by a larger, better equipped opponent.

She smiled as she made her decision. It was time to visit another friend of her father's. A friend, unlike John, she could be sure of, based on her personal experience. After the safe-deposit box went back into the vault, she booked herself on the next available flight to Chicago. Victoria Colby-Camp could help her.

# Chapter Three

*Chicago, 5:30 p.m.*

Frankie had fond memories of visiting with "Aunt Victoria," though it was an honorary title. Somewhere in a box she had yet to unpack in Savannah, there was a framed photo of her with Victoria at a Fourth of July barbecue. When news of her father's suicide flooded the media, Victoria had been one of the few people who'd sent her a sympathy card.

The evidence of her mother's betrayal burned through her system as Frankie sat in Victoria's reception area. She wanted advice on how to proceed. Sophia couldn't be allowed to get away with this.

Frankie shifted in the chair. It was a nice enough piece of furniture, for someone who hadn't spent too many hours on airplanes recently. She needed to take a break to stretch and let her back recover, but she had no time to waste. All the physical therapy in the world couldn't change the simple fact that she wouldn't rest easy until this was over.

The receptionist stationed outside Victoria's office directed Frankie to the coffee service, and she had barely declined when Victoria opened her office door. Frankie smiled. The woman still looked as regal as she remembered. Though her dark hair was now streaked with gray, Victoria remained beautiful.

"Frankie, what a pleasure to see you again." She crossed the room and gave her a warm hug. "It's been far too long. How are you feeling?"

"Fit as ever, though the navy docs didn't clear me for active duty."

"That's frustrating," Victoria said, guiding her into the office and closing the door behind them. "Have a seat and tell me how things are going. I hear you joined the Savannah Police Department."

Frankie smiled. "As an analyst," she replied, though she was sure Victoria knew that, as well. It would've been more surprising if Victoria hadn't checked into her background. "It's good work and I enjoy it."

"But not as exciting as your previous career."

"Few things are," Frankie agreed.

"Your message sounded quite urgent," Victoria said, concern in her eyes.

"It is. Thanks for seeing me."

Frankie had rehearsed the talking points on the flight and refined them in the cab. Now her stomach clenched. Maybe she should've taken more time to review the flash drive first. No, the statement alone was damaging enough to enlist Victoria's opinion and guidance. "I need some advice," she began.

*Just start at the beginning and walk through it step by step*, she coached herself. She was more convinced than ever that her mother had been part of the plan to railroad her father. What baffled her was why. And rushing straight to that conclusion without the backstory would get her nowhere. Victoria was her last chance.

"I'm glad you came to me," the older woman said, her voice soothing.

"You knew my parents well?"

She nodded. "I knew them both, long before they married."

"Did you follow their careers?"

"Not particularly. Mainly what they shared in Christmas cards or when your father made the news." Victoria reached for her cup of coffee. "For his successes."

Frankie rubbed her palms on her jeans, wishing she'd worn the one dress she'd packed for this trip. Her soft green sweater set felt too casual next to Victoria's polished style, and Frankie felt absolutely outclassed by the elegantly furnished office. Everything screamed experience and expertise. Which was why she was here. "I don't know who else to turn to," she admitted. "I found evidence that my mother lied to me about my father's case, and probably several other things, as well," she added, thinking of the passports.

Victoria set her coffee aside. "What sort of evidence?"

Frankie pulled the statement from the envelope in her backpack. Handing it over, she explained, "Sophia had a choice and she willingly contributed to his guilty verdict."

"Sophia?" Victoria echoed with an arching eyebrow. She studied Frankie over the top of the document. "You actually believe that."

"I've suspected it for some time," Frankie replied. "You're holding the proof."

Victoria picked up a pair of glasses and set them in place to read the statement. When she finished, she placed the papers gingerly on her desktop, as though they might explode. "How did you get this?"

"A friend of Dad's came to see me. He gave me a key to a safe-deposit box and warned me the contents could be dangerous. That document was one of several items inside."

"Go on."

"False passports with Sophia's picture, a flash drive with more information that connects her to my father's death, and other personal items from Dad."

"Did you recognize this friend?"

"No," Frankie admitted. She pulled out her phone and brought up the pictures she'd taken at the diner. "Do you? He told me he was close to my parents."

Victoria adjusted her glasses and carefully examined each photo. "I've never seen him. You should speak with your mother and verify your source and the accuracy of this statement."

"I have." Frankie swallowed her impatience. "Well, I haven't asked her about this man, but we've talked about Dad. Argued really. Her answers weren't clear or helpful. Or even honest, in light of all this."

"Frankie. You've been part of covert operations. It's a world of smoke and mirrors. You know reports rarely give the full picture of any situation."

"You won't help me get to the truth?"

Victoria sighed. "What are you asking me to do?"

Frankie wanted to get up and pace or scream,

or otherwise release some of the frustration building inside her. Instead, she remained in the chair. "I have nightmares about my dad's downfall and death. He wasn't a traitor." She stopped and swallowed when her voice started to crack. "I can't believe it, not about the man I knew."

"Frankie—"

"I know I'm looking at this with a daughter's eyes. I talked with Sophia several times when he was accused and after they found him guilty. She was too composed through the whole mess. Never a tear or any sign of worry. What kind of wife doesn't worry when her husband is accused of treason?" Frankie paused, pulling on the tattered edges of her composure. Losing it would get her nowhere. "Sophia never gave me anything but the same tired reply—trust the process."

"It's sound advice."

"It didn't work." Frankie left out the irrelevant piece that trusting a legal process included zero comfort factor. "It was a self-serving answer," she argued. "Suicide isn't part of any fair or just process. How did he even manage that with the security team that must have been surrounding him?"

Frankie took a moment to compose herself. "Aunt Victoria, I have a new job, I'm making

a new life, but I haven't moved on. Not really."
She scooted to the edge of the chair. "I need the
answers. I deserve to know what happened and
who I can trust. There's no way I can move forward until I clear up the past."

"I understand how that feels," Victoria said,
her words heavy with the wisdom of experience. "But leaping to conclusions will only hurt
you. Others, too, most likely. I've known your
mother a very long time. Her word should be
enough for you."

"What word? She won't explain herself,"
Frankie pressed, desperate for Victoria's help.
"My father's been silenced. I want to understand
what happened."

"You want revenge," Victoria stated bluntly.
"Who will you target and what price will you
pay?"

Frankie forced herself to calm down, taking
a deep breath and releasing it slowly. "My dad
isn't a traitor. Even dead, he doesn't deserve to
bear that notoriety." She fidgeted in the chair,
wishing again she could get up and pace. "Apparently the friend of his who found me yesterday is the only person who agrees with me."

"You don't know that." Victoria tapped the
papers in front of her. "This statement doesn't
prove your mother was complicit if there *was* a
concerted effort to ruin your father. She had to

make an accurate report. Her position and her integrity required it."

"It's *not* accurate. Dad was in Bagram when she stated he was in Kabul." Frankie hadn't felt so helpless since she'd woken in a hospital bed with no feeling in her legs. She needed an ally. Just as the candid support of the medical team had empowered her recovery, one trustworthy partner would make all the difference now.

Victoria's eyes lit with troubled interest. "How can you be sure?"

"Because I was there. I saw him." She nearly cheered when Victoria's brow furrowed as she reviewed the report again.

"Let me see the passports."

Frankie handed them over and endured the small eternity awaiting Victoria's response.

The older woman reached for her phone and pressed a button. "Ask Aidan to join us, please." She replaced the handset and met Frankie's gaze. "Aidan Abbot is one of my best investigators. No one's better with documents or ferreting through layers of security or fraud. He can tell us if the passports are fakes."

"How could they possibly be real?"

Victoria flipped through the pages. "Frankie, you know there are times when an established alias is necessary. Or all of this could be an elaborate setup to turn you against her."

"I've already been against her for months. We haven't spoken since his funeral." An event that had been postponed a full month so Frankie could attend. Too bad it hadn't made anything easier. The delay had only given her mother more time to pretend life with her spouse hadn't existed. The brutal lack of emotion had shocked Frankie. Still did. If Sophia so willingly cut out a husband, losing a daughter probably hadn't registered on her scale. Everything Frankie thought she knew about love and family had been turned upside down by a disaster someone had manufactured. Hurting, her blood beating cold in her veins, Frankie fixed her gaze on the window and the city glittering beyond it.

"Let's assume you're right," Victoria continued. "It would require serious planning and resources to systematically take down a man of your father's standing. To create evidence strong enough to ruin his career and push him to suicide without leaving a trail would be almost impossible these days."

A knock sounded on the door. Frankie turned to see it open and a man with thick, dark hair in need of a trim, and vivid, cobalt-blue eyes, enter.

"Aidan Abbot, Francesca Leone."

"A pleasure," he said, shaking her hand.

There was a trace of Ireland in his voice and

it sent her pulse into some foolish feminine skipping. He probably got that all the time, she thought, irritated with her reaction. "Likewise," she replied.

"Francesca's a lovely name."

The way he said it made her want to sigh and forget why she'd come here. She cleared her throat. "Call me Frankie." She'd been named in honor of both her grandmother and father. Her full name had always felt too exotic. "Frankie" was a better fit for the tough and proud little girl who'd spent her life aspiring to be like her dad.

When he was seated, Victoria handed Aidan the passports. "Frankie has some concerns about these."

Frankie watched him examine them, involuntarily admiring his hands, as well as his attention to detail. More annoying was the difficulty she seemed to be having with the fact that he wore some appealing cologne that reminded her of the Pacific Coast on a clear, sunny day.

"One woman with two names implies that one of them is a fake," he said after a moment.

"Both are fakes," Frankie stated firmly.

Aidan arched a dark eyebrow, and his mouth quirked up at one corner. Frankie felt a warm tremor just under her skin. It was a relief when he turned that bold blue gaze toward his boss. "If there's no question, why call me?"

"There may be good reason those passports were issued. Would you mind taking a closer look into the names and any travel records?"

"Not at all." He tapped the closed passports against his knee. "How much time do I have?"

"A few hours at most," Victoria said, her eyes cool. "Frankie wants the information yesterday."

Frankie couldn't sit still a moment longer. Her back ached from the travel and the tension. She wanted the freedom and clarity of a quick run but settled for pacing the width of the office. The patience she'd relied on in the field and in her work didn't translate to this situation. "That's a start. Can you tell me what sort of legal action we can take?" She shoved her hands into her pockets.

"Why don't you give me what you have?" Victoria suggested. "Let my team investigate while you go back to Savannah. We're good, objective and fast. I'll call you as soon as we know something."

Frankie shook her head, her ponytail swinging. "I'm not sitting this one out." She'd been relegated to the sidelines too often since her injury. While she couldn't say she knew her parents better than anyone—the opposite appeared to be true—she wouldn't deal with this long-distance via secondhand reports. She wanted to see her mother's face when the truth finally came out.

"Then why did you come to me?"

She felt Aidan's gaze on her as Victoria waited for an answer. Frankie wished she could ask him to leave. She didn't want to share the ugly Leone family secrets with a stranger. "For support and guidance," she replied, keeping her gaze on Victoria. "I took vacation through next week. I'll go to Seattle and confront my mother about that statement while you investigate the passports and other documents. Won't that be enough time to know if we have a case against her?"

"Frankie—"

"I'll tell her I want to reconcile, to mend the rift," Frankie explained. "Hopefully, she'll buy it and open up. If that isn't enough, I'll ask for a job. Anything to lower her defenses."

Victoria glanced at Aidan. "Frankie's mother owns Leo Solutions, a security firm in Seattle."

"Cyber or personal?" Aidan inquired.

"Both, if I understand the setup," Frankie answered. "She and her business partner built it on the backs of their government careers." Regretting her burst of bitterness, she plowed on. "Once I'm out there, I thought I'd worm my way past her defenses. With your agency working this behind the scenes and me working on-site, I'm sure we can get to the truth quickly."

"Frankie." Victoria leaned back in her chair, her reading glasses in her hands. "Going out there with the intent to deceive your mother is a terrible risk."

Frankie paused, studying her. "I've worked undercover before." She couldn't afford to think of this as anything other than a mission. If her mother could ignore the bonds of family, so could she.

"That's not what I mean. Please, sit down."

Reluctantly, Frankie returned to her chair. She didn't want to endure a lecture on discretion or family unity in front of Aidan, but it seemed Victoria wasn't giving her a choice.

"Since I clearly can't stop you from going, I'm sending Aidan with you."

"Pardon me?" Having braced for the lecture, Frankie needed a moment to digest the actual statement. "That's not necessary." She shot a quick look in Aidan's direction. "Can't he research the passports and documents from here?"

"I want him on-site," Victoria said. "You shouldn't be out there alone."

"I'll keep you updated—" Frankie began.

"I know you will," she interrupted. "That isn't the point. I refuse to take any chances with your safety." She turned to her computer monitor, and her hands rattled on her keyboard for a moment. Then she met Frankie's gaze with a thoughtful expression. "Assuming your mother's statement is legitimate, your search will likely lead to someone better prepared to retaliate than offer up a confession."

Yes, Frankie was angry and she was hurt. That didn't make her a fool. "I've considered that and taken precautions." She didn't want or need a babysitter. The fewer witnesses to her family embarrassments, the better.

"Good," Victoria replied.

"You know I can protect myself."

"This isn't up for debate, Frankie. I've known you since you were a child. You'll give your mom a call and let her know you're coming out for a visit. We'll get Aidan an interview with your mother's company by Monday afternoon." She held up a hand when Frankie started to protest again. "I'm sure he'll be hired. As former Interpol, he knows his way around security and covert operations. Once the details are settled, the two of you can work together."

*Call her mom?* She wasn't a teenager caught smoking in the girls' room. Her mother wouldn't believe Frankie suddenly had an urge for mother-daughter bonding time, and Frankie wanted the element of surprise. "That's not—"

Victoria cut her off. "I *insist* that you have

someone watching your back." Standing, she came around the desk and pulled Frankie to her feet for another hug. When she let go, her eyes were misty. "Legal debacles and strained relationships aside, try to focus on the things your parents did right. They gave you their love and affection through a wonderful childhood. Both of them raised a strong, independent woman."

Frankie did her best to muster a smile as the grief sliced through her. She'd questioned every nuance of her life lately, wondering what to believe about her parents and how that impacted her view of herself. Cornerstones of her upbringing seemed little more than loose theories in light of recent events. "I'll be careful," she repeated, not wanting to lie to Victoria.

"I hope your mother helps you find what you're after." The woman's smile was sad. "Would you like us to stay while you make the call?"

Frankie hesitated, but only for a moment. If this investigator would be trailing her around Seattle, he might as well get a taste of what he was in for. He'd be combing through her family's secrets soon enough.

AIDAN DID HIS best impersonation of an invisible man while Frankie spoke briefly with her mother. It was clear she wasn't happy about Victoria's insistence on the task, but his boss was difficult to outmaneuver. Her voice cool and her face pale, Frankie managed a polite exchange, excusing herself from the office the moment it was over.

"The woman's a spitfire," he observed, closing the door behind her. He admired her grit. Not to mention her lush sable hair, expressive dark eyes and that generous mouth. Even without the surname Leone tipping him off, her perfect posture implied a military background. Although with those cheekbones and long limbs, she could've passed as a model. If she wasn't a new client, he might have asked her out for a drink. "I'm to get myself hired and then what?"

"Find a way to stay close to her. If the documents are real, she'll be a target as soon as the person pulling the strings learns she found them. I want you there. You're the best at unraveling knots like this one."

That was Victoria's way of saying she suspected fraud, his primary focus during his time with Interpol. "Do I report to you only?" The freedom and case variation were nice, though his favorite part of being a Colby investigator was the concise chain of command.

"Yes, please. I don't care for the way she was led to what she considers proof positive her mother willfully ended her father's career. The only thing I believe about the man who dropped this in her lap is that digging for the truth could get her hurt. Or worse."

"Yes, ma'am." Aidan waited for the other shoe to drop.

"General Leone was an excellent strategist," Victoria said, almost to herself. "Frankie takes after him. She's smart and highly skilled, but I'm afraid she's rejecting the most logical explanation. It's understandable under the circumstances. I'm sure you heard the temper and need for vengeance in her voice."

He bobbed his chin. "Hard to miss."

"Please tread lightly," Victoria continued. "As you meet Sophia Leone and work out the details with Frankie, keep an open mind. You might be the only one who can."

"Of course." At least in this case he wasn't at the center of the storm battering the family. There was a great deal of comfort in that.

"I'll send you her file for review," Victoria said, leaning back against her desk. "The most pertinent fact is Frankie's service as a cultural liaison with the navy SEALs."

That gave Aidan pause. Though it was the only post women could fill on those operations, very few had the tenacity and fortitude to do so.

"She looks a little young to have hit her twenty years already."

"She suffered a serious injury while her team was in a convoy that left her paralyzed for a time. Inconveniently, her recovery coincided with her father's problems. Surgery and months of rehab got her walking again, but the navy retired her for medical reasons."

That explained some of the anger, Aidan thought. He knew firsthand it was never easy to relinquish control when life dealt out an unexpected detour.

"She claims she's fit," Victoria added, "but I'm not entirely convinced."

"Duly noted," Aidan said. Healthy and able-bodied weren't the same as fit for service. If this case turned into a danger zone, he'd offer protection first and apologize for any insult later.

"Expect her to try to shake you."

He'd already reached the same assumption. "Do you think she'll blow my cover?"

"No. She wants the truth too much to take that chance. That doesn't mean she'll cooperate with you."

"She's not my first challenging case," he reminded his boss.

Victoria blessed him with an amused smile. "I was right to call you in on this one."

"I'll see her safely through whatever happens," he promised.

"Thank you. It's the least I owe her parents."

A firm knock sounded on the door and Victoria signaled for him to open it. He did, finding Frankie on the other side, her dark eyes sparking with impatience. She marched right past him to confront Victoria. "Your receptionist tells me she's booking us on a flight to Seattle tomorrow."

Aidan took a position that gave him the best view of the inevitable fireworks.

"That's right," Victoria said. "I'm not taking any chances, and you told me you didn't want to waste any more time."

"I need to go home first," Frankie replied. "I'll travel from there."

Victoria folded her arms across her chest. "Do you think your mother hasn't kept tabs on you? Traveling from Savannah gains you nothing. Sophia and I are friends. She might very well call me for advice about *you*. We've both had challenges with children."

Frankie didn't cooperate with the clear dismissal. "That's not it," she protested.

Victoria tapped her reading glasses against her palm. "Are you having second thoughts?"

*Brick, meet wall*, Aidan thought, watching the two women.

"No."

The internal battle Frankie was obviously waging dragged out for another long minute. She still didn't explain herself. Aidan caught Victoria's eye. "Frankie." He waited for her to turn his way. "Any gear you might want you can borrow from us. I'll show you the way."

Behind Frankie, he caught Victoria's relieved expression when the younger woman finally agreed, slinging her backpack over one shoulder and retrieving her suitcase. When they were alone in the elevator, he felt a modicum of tension ease. He asked what she expected to find in Seattle.

"I'm trying not to expect much of anything," she answered.

"That limits the potential disappointment." He'd walked through life a long while with that mind-set. "And the potential happiness."

She sighed, her hand flexing on the strap of her backpack. "I know I must sound like an overgrown toddler on the verge of a tantrum."

That wasn't what he saw at all. He saw a woman in pain, confused and wary. "I don't know enough about your situation to have an opinion."

She looked up at him and laughed, the startled, bright sound bouncing around the elevator car and spilling out as the doors parted. "Oh, you have an opinion," she said. "Maybe I'll ask for it later."

He didn't want to be fascinated by this new client with a huge chip on her shoulder, yet he couldn't quite stop himself. She exuded stubbornness, and he couldn't imagine what kind of strength required to overcome her injuries.

As an investigator, he was naturally curious about all the things she hadn't said, but it certainly didn't help his concentration that she made such an art form out of walking.

# Chapter Four

Aidan watched Frankie carefully choose a laptop and a cell phone to back up the devices she'd brought along. Together they decided on surveillance gear, both visual and audible, proving she understood the tech. He nearly laughed out loud, thinking he'd met the perfect woman. It was a relief that he couldn't act on the undercurrent of attraction teasing his senses. He was more than capable of working with beautiful women as partners and clients, and he'd sworn off ever bridging the gap between business and personal again.

As she examined some newer button cameras, he picked up a surveillance-signal jammer. When they moved toward the available weapons, he selected a 9 mm semiautomatic and a .22 revolver as backup, along with ammunition. Frankie shied away from all of them.

"No?" How was it possible an American with her background didn't carry a gun?

She shook her head, her pretty eyes clouded with something he couldn't quite label. "I prefer knives."

*Knives?* Was that some strange holdover from her navy days? "You brought knives? We're flying commercial."

"It'll be okay," she replied confidently. "I flew commercial to get here."

"Can I see them?"

She arched one dark eyebrow before consenting to rest her backpack on the table. "If you can find them." She stepped back, crossed her arms and waited.

He searched the main compartments, but other than her laptop, phone and a variety of other personal items, he found only her multipurpose tool and a digital camera no bigger than his palm. He patted every inch of the material, searching for a blade in a hidden pocket, until he finally admitted defeat.

With a shake of her head, she unzipped the main pocket once more and reached to the bottom. Then he heard the distinctive tear of a hook-and-loop pouch opening. A moment later, she revealed a black clip point, fixed-blade knife.

"That doesn't look like standard navy issue," he said.

She shrugged, a gleam of pride shining in her eyes. "It's what I carried when we deployed."

Any doubts he'd had about her military pedigree evaporated. "Won't do you much good in a gunfight," he pointed out.

With another hitch of her shoulders, she tucked it out of sight. "Haven't you heard? I'm not heading to a gunfight. I'm heading for a happy reunion with my mom."

She didn't sound the least bit happy.

"Why do you prefer a knife over a gun?" Aidan asked.

"It's easier to get through airport security. Easier to conceal no matter what I'm wearing. And I don't need a permit."

Considering the lethal-looking blade, he wasn't so sure he could agree with any of her reasons. "How *did* you get it through security?"

"The pocket is a double layer of ballistic fabric. Unless they know where to look and how to open it, it's invisible to a security scan."

"Nice trick," he admitted.

"How do you get the guns through?"

"Registrations and permits in checked baggage. The private investigator license helps, too," he added as he gathered up the gear. "How do you think your mom will react when you're on her doorstep?"

"I'm not sure." Frankie looked at a small button camera on the end of a pen. "At least we have gadgets and tools on our side. It feels like a spy movie set in here."

He laughed. He'd thought the same thing when he first arrived. "Victoria keeps us well equipped. She has a reputation as the best."

"That she does," Frankie said quietly. "You knew of it even at Interpol?"

"Yes." He could practically see the wheels turning inside her head. She'd been more than uncomfortable at the end of the meeting, pushing against Victoria's control of the investigation. He should've seen it earlier. Frankie had felt cornered and outnumbered, possibly even betrayed. She'd done what was necessary to get through it and out of the office, retreating but not relinquishing anything just yet. It made her a hazard—to both of them.

"You can trust her," he said, knowing he'd hit the mark when her gaze snapped to his. "And me, by extension."

"Sure." She looked around, studying every-thing but him. "Are we done here?"

"Pretty much." He checked his phone. "Flight reservations are booked. We're on a midmorn-ing flight."

"Not the early one?" She reached for her own cell phone even as she leaned to look over his shoulder.

When she was this close, the ginger and clove scents of her hair teased his senses. He ignored the enticing aroma, the way it slid over and around him, in favor of keeping her talking. "Please tell me you're not a crack-of-dawn type of person," he said with exaggerated fear.

Her eyebrows puckered. "Why do you care? It's not as though we'll be living together." Then her mouth formed a perfect circle. "Oh. Victoria's orders?" She flicked those away with a twitch of her fingers. "Don't worry about playing bodyguard. I can handle myself. As long as we find time and space to check in regularly about the case, you won't have to follow me around."

It was far too early to throw himself on that conversational grenade. "Are you up for a review of the situation before we call it a night?"

"Sure." The tight curve of her lips hardly qualified as a smile. "It will give us more time on-site to scope out the area before we knock on her door."

He couldn't argue with Frankie's work ethic. "We can talk in the conference room."

"Great." Her smile carried little enthusiasm. He wondered how her face and eyes might get in on the action if she ever smiled sincerely. Her outward calm didn't quite cover all the anger lurking underneath. He wanted a look at the evidence so he could gain some insight and perspective. Until he had a better grasp of the situation, her tension made him edgy, as well. Too bad he couldn't blame it all on mutual attraction, but that seemed to be entirely his problem. If she noticed him as anything other than an interloper, she hid it well.

"I'd like to learn all I can so I'm prepared to recon your happy reunion, and know the right words for my interview on Monday."

With a small nod, she trailed him to the elevator, her suitcase rolling along behind them. When the lift arrived, they stepped inside and he punched the button for the conference room. They decided on a pizza from a little place down the street, and he set about searching through what she knew and what she thought she knew about her mom.

An aerial view of Sophia's neighborhood and the surrounding blocks filled one of the computer monitors. "When you meet with your mother, I'll watch the house from right here," he said, pointing to a corner he'd highlighted.

"Are you worried I'll do something stupid?" Frankie gave him a long look.

He stared right back. "Are you planning on doing something stupid?"

She tilted her head to the side, stretching and massaging the long column of her neck. "Of course not."

Did she know she was irresistible? "Here." He stepped behind her. "Let me."

She shifted out of his reach. "No, thanks."

"No problem." He held his hands up in surrender. Though he was tempted to fib and tell her he was a certified massage therapist, he didn't want to give her any reason to doubt his word. In the short time they'd been acquainted, her trust issues were abundantly clear.

"It's just from the plane," she said defensively. "I tweaked it when I dozed off."

"It happens." He kept his smile easy, his stance casual. "If you change your mind, I've picked up a trick or two from my massage therapist sister." That was the truth.

"Rain check." Frankie looked back at the overhead images of the neighborhood. "If you're going to watch the first meeting, I assume you'll want me wired for sound, too?"

He was glad she'd been the one to suggest it. "If you agree, we could analyze the conversation afterward for any slips or stresses she makes."

"She won't slip up. Sophia Leone is too slick, too careful."

Aidan thought it was possible the apple hadn't fallen far from the Leone family tree. Frankie appeared to be an extremely cautious woman, as well. Whether it was nature or circumstance, he could honor that trait, respect it. He needed to earn her trust quickly, for everyone's benefit. "Once you're reunited, you'll have better personal access, and I can be looking for anything within the company records, associates or systems that implicate her or clear her of wrongdoing."

Frankie nodded, but he knew her mind was working overtime on something she wasn't ready to share. Leo Solutions had gone from idea to full-service business in a remarkably short time. That required significant capital, though Frankie blamed the instant growth on her mother's extensive connections. He'd withhold his opinion until he had more information.

He didn't discuss his reasons, simply made a list and kept digging. Sophia Leone's personal finances were remarkably transparent. She'd tucked the money from the general's death into a trust fund for their daughter. A fund Frankie refused to touch. Considering the salary Sophia drew from the company, she lived modestly and seemed to be socking away as much as possible into savings. This piqued his curiosity.

"Did you ever discuss your personal goals for after your service with your mom?"

"No," Frankie said, distracted by her study of her mother's neighborhood. "I was on active duty one day and retired the next. The transition time was filled with physical therapy." She zoomed out and moved the cursor to the Leo Solutions site. "Why did you leave Interpol?"

"Victoria made me a better offer." She had, in fact, saved more than his career when she invited him into the Colby Agency.

"Sounds like there's a story." Frankie shot him a sideways glance under her lashes.

That look landed like a punch to his gut, stealing his breath. "Isn't there always in our line of work?" If she wanted to hear it, he'd share a few of the more palatable details. He waited, relieved when she didn't ask.

Pushing herself out of her chair, she rolled her shoulders and then pressed her fists into her back. "I passed the physical," she said with a weary frown. "It's the new hardware in my spine the navy can't accept. You don't have to worry about me breaking on your watch."

"I wasn't thinking about that at all." He'd been thinking far less appropriate things about the gentle flare of her hips and the supple way she moved.

"You'd be the first."

"Will you tell me how you got hurt?" He needed to find some common ground, a starting point they could build from. He had no intention of being the first of Victoria's investigators to go down in flames before a client left the building.

"It was an improvised explosive at the edge of a dirt track too vague and rutted to qualify as a road." Her voice was as quiet and still as a pond sheltered by a bank of fog. "They tell me I was tossed up in the air like a doll. It was the landing I screwed up."

He marveled that she could be almost meditative about such a life-altering event. The contrast between her distrust and temper over her father's demise and her serenity about her personal troubles intrigued him. His injuries had been emotional, though the alcohol required to silence his demons had taken a toll. "You don't remember it?"

"Not the explosion." She stacked her hands on top of her head. "I remember far too much of the recovery." She glanced up at the clock on the wall. "It's late. I really wish I could've gone home first."

He understood the subject was closed. For now. "What did you leave behind?"

"Clothes. I didn't pack for a week of socializing with my mom. She's always perfectly dressed for any moment. You'll see."

He wasn't buying that. What did he have to do to earn a peek into her real concerns? "You're not going to shake me," he said. "We're going from here to the hotel, to the airport. We're catching the flight into Seattle tomorrow. You can shop there if it becomes a problem."

She studied him, her big brown eyes impossible to read. "I don't want to shake you." Her gaze dropped to his lips. A long moment later, she glared at the computer as she shut it down. "Do I call a cab to get to the hotel or are you in charge of my every move?"

He grinned at her, noted her irritation. "We'll go together and call it team building."

"Team?" She snorted. "You'll be asking for a trade as soon as you meet Sophia Leone and get caught up on the fiasco that is my family."

Aidan didn't reply. Once he took a case, he stuck until it was closed. No matter what.

*Saturday, April 9, 8:20 a.m.*

AIDAN COUNTED IT a victory when they arrived at the airport on time and without further argument or conflict. When they were seated on the plane, he quickly changed his mind. The seats were too close, her body one temptation after another as she carefully situated herself and her belongings.

More than the fleeting, innocent touches of her arm or knee, the way her mind worked—swift and a little dark—compounded his problem. She was a *client* and deserved his best effort on the case. He had to find a way to ignore how she stirred him. More, he had to find a way to ignore the brief, assessing glances she'd been aiming his direction when she thought he wasn't looking.

They'd been at peak altitude for just over an hour when she shifted in her seat. "Aidan?"

Her hair was down today and as she pushed it behind her ear he caught that lovely scent again. "Yes?"

"I'm thinking we need to change up the plan."

He kept his expression neutral, though he couldn't wait to hear what she'd been mulling over since last night. "How so?"

"If we go into Leo Solutions separately, the odds aren't in our favor. Either one of us could get tossed out if we're discovered. This may be my best chance to learn the truth. I can't afford to get pushed back to square one."

"You don't have much faith in me, do you?"

"It's not that." She twisted more, her knee bumping his. "We're walking into a security company. They're going to find out we were on the same plane, that we sat together."

"That won't be a problem," he said. The problem would be keeping his hands to himself if he didn't find some distance.

"It's too coincidental. We should go on the offensive."

He had a sudden image of Frankie charging ahead, leading a strike team, heedless of the American military rules about women in combat. "Dare I ask what you have in mind?"

She gave him a smile and it stunned him. No falsehood in this smile, no tension, just pure excitement. The expression lit her eyes and brought a hint of color to her cheeks. For a moment he was lost to anything but the gorgeous view.

"Rather than wait for them to confront us," she was saying, "why don't we just go in together?"

"We are going in together." Sitting together on the plane didn't have to be a big deal. For the case.

"No, together like a *couple*," she said, her dark eyes sparkling. "Let's tell Sophia we're engaged."

He stared at her, dumbfounded, while she hurried to explain.

"Hear me out. My mom's a big romantic. Always has been." Frankie's smile evaporated. "One more reason it baffles me that she tossed her soul mate under the bus," she added in a low voice. "If we show up and tell her we're engaged, we effectively distract her."

This was a bad idea. Horrible. "I don't—"

"I've thought it through," Frankie promised, cutting him off. "We'll tell her you applied to the company and when you got the interview on your own merit we decided to come out and surprise her with the whole truth. She'll eat it up."

"She'll see right through it," he argued.

"Not a chance. We'll tell her it's been a long-distance thing and we can't stand living apart anymore. This is perfect, trust me." Frankie nearly bounced in her seat.

His stomach pitched and rolled as if they were going through severe turbulence. "What about the living arrangements?"

"What about them? Being engaged gives us the perfect reason to talk to each other anytime we want through the workday or in the evenings. We won't need any excuses. It's a stronger plan all around."

It didn't feel that way to him. He had to convince her to drop it. "The plan was a hotel room for me and you in the house with your mom."

"Yeah…" Frankie shook her head, and the sable waves of her hair rippled. "No matter what we decide about this, I won't stay with her."

"It gives you tremendous access."

"Access or not, I can't do it." She tucked her

hands between her thighs as if she were suddenly cold. "I've lived on my own too long. We'd be snapping at each other before I found out anything useful."

"We need to stick with the plan and cover Victoria arranged," he said, willing her to be reasonable. He couldn't be engaged. Not even for a case. "This kind of change should be approved." There, he'd found a point she couldn't argue with.

"What does it matter, if we get the job done?" Frankie countered. "This tactic simplifies everything."

Maybe for her. His fingers cramped into a fist, digging into his palm. This couldn't be happening. He wouldn't give in.

"Arriving engaged is the best answer," she said, patting his knee as if the topic was settled.

"No," he murmured, glancing around for anyone who might've caught their conversation. "I won't alter the op without approval."

She snorted. "Please. Victoria knows things change and investigators have to think on their feet. Let's make the most of it."

He shook his head and looked past her to the sky flying by the window. This was ridiculous.

"Is it such an impossible task to pretend to like me when we're in public?"

"Of course not," he replied. He was afraid

how easy it would be to treat her as a fiancée. "It changes the dynamic. Significantly. Lying as part of a cover is one thing. Lying to each other is another."

"What do you mean?" Her dark eyebrows dipped into another sharp frown. "We'll be lying to the suspect, not to each other."

"Only in public," he said with a hefty dose of sarcasm. He hadn't missed how she'd termed her mother as a suspect. "Being engaged typically means affectionate displays and exhibiting a sense of closeness and trust." He leaned closer and she leaned away, proving his point.

"Are you afraid I'm going to forget it's for show and fall in love with you?" She rolled her eyes. "Please. I'm not prowling for a relationship, Aidan. Let's agree to do whatever it takes to get the job done efficiently."

He eased back into his seat, letting her believe she'd put him in his place. "Let me think it over." He flipped open his tablet and continued his study of the Leone family background.

"Just decide before we land," she whispered.

He didn't reply. Her need for control was likely a combination of her upbringing, her natural fiery personality and the career-ending injury. He couldn't blame her for that. He did, however, want to look at her "proposal" from all angles, especially from her mother's point of view.

He wasn't worried about his family finding out. In Ireland, they were all well away from any gossip, and the agency should be intercepting any queries. No, he was more concerned about how he'd feel playing Frankie's groom-to-be, even if only for a few days. He prided himself on being able to roll with the unexpected elements of his work. Surely there was a way to talk her out of this.

Eventually, he closed his tablet and reached over to take her hand.

"What are you doing?" She tugged, but he held on.

"Holding my fiancée's hand." This would be his ticket back to the sane side of this case.

"Oh." Her fingers relaxed a fraction. "You agree then that this is the best avenue to take?"

"I'm weighing the pros and cons."

Her brown eyes narrowed and her intelligent gaze turned suspicious. "I outlined the only pros that matter."

"To you."

"Aidan." She jerked her hand free of his. "What are you thinking?"

He grinned at the wariness in her eyes. She couldn't possibly want to play this out, not the way they needed to, to make it convincing. "I really don't think the fake engagement is the best way to go."

"Why not?" Lacing her fingers together, she balanced her hands on her slim thigh. Her brown eyes lit with a challenge and her foot began to tap. "Afraid you're not up to it?"

*On the contrary.* Faking an intimacy would be too easy with Frankie. His attraction for her was already cranked up and getting hotter by the minute. In other circumstances, with the slightest encouragement from her, he'd have made his move. When she gazed up at him, he could see flecks of gold in her brown eyes. He forced himself to take a mental step back rather than lean across the arm of the seat and crowd her personal space. "You're an only child, right?"

She nodded.

"If you show up on your mom's doorstep with a fiancé in tow, she's going to go ballistic with excitement."

"That's the *point*." Frankie waved off the idea that it was a bad thing. "I haven't spoken a word to her in months. The engagement diverts her suspicion about showing up now. What do you care if she gushes over you? It's a week, tops. More likely she'll be walking on eggshells, afraid to intrude in my personal life."

He wasn't nearly so sure. Sophia Leone didn't

strike him as the selfish, remorseless woman Frankie thought she was. "I believe you're underestimating her," he pressed. Specifically, Sophia's love for and commitment to her only child. "Our original story is strong enough without the complication of a false engagement."

"Is there someone else?" Frankie demanded suddenly. "A girlfriend or wife who'd be offended by our plan?"

"Your plan," he corrected. "And no."

"Then discussion over."

"Not so fast." Leaning close, he caught that sweet scent of cloves and spices in her hair. "Are you prepared to play the part…*completely*?"

He watched her, relentlessly quelling his grin as her eyes went wide when his full meaning registered. It was gratifying to realize she wasn't immune to this electricity humming between them. He pulled himself together. The last thing he needed was to play with fire on a case Victoria had a personal interest in. He had to show Frankie this ploy was a mistake.

She moistened her lips. "Are you prepared?"

"Of course," he replied automatically. "I always go the distance in my investigations."

"And in other areas?"

"Are you flirting with me?"

She batted her eyes in an exaggerated move that made him laugh, until she closed the distance and pressed her lips to his. Warmth spread from that point of contact down his arms, sizzling in his fingertips. She pushed her hand into his hair and drew him closer for a full, sensual kiss that blasted through him like a flash grenade.

She was like a double shot of whiskey with a drop of honey—all fire with a hint of sweetness. He changed the angle, tipping up her chin and taking control of the kiss. When her lips parted on a sigh, he slid his tongue across hers with bold strokes.

Belatedly he remembered the plane full of people and eased away. Her eyes were dazed, a mirror of his own, he was sure. "I think that will convince anyone." It sure as hell convinced him.

He prayed it would be enough to put an end to her irrational engagement idea.

# Chapter Five

Frankie reached for the magazine, though she'd read it cover to cover already. It annoyed her no end that her hands shook. She could still taste the cola Aidan had chosen during the beverage service. The hint of crisp pine in his cologne tickled her nose and made her think of the rocky coast near Puget Sound.

Maybe he was right and pretending an engagement was the wrong move.

If that shocking kiss was any indication— even though she had started it—she'd have to be very careful. If they had to do much of that, it would be all too easy to believe the charade intended to knock down her mother's defenses.

Thoughts of her mom killed the lingering sizzle from the kiss. Sophia had boasted about keeping that spark of love and romance alive through thirty years of marriage. Obviously that had been one more lie on top of the heap. Her statement, all but convicting her husband, left no room for anything but the clear conclusion: Sophia's career had trumped love in the end. She must have turned against her husband to avoid the demolition of her career by association. How would her security business have succeeded if shadowed by General Leone's treason?

Distracting her mother was worth any personal discomfort to Frankie. The announcement that she and Aidan were engaged would give them a brief advantage, and Frankie planned to make the most of it.

She pressed her lips together, telling herself it was silly the way her heartbeat skipped when he touched her. It was true he could be her fantasy man come to life with his dark looks, quick smile and vivid blue eyes. And the accent? Dear God. Too bad this was absolutely the wrong time in her life. She had to find a way to deal with it if they were going to convince Sophia they were engaged.

Frankie had to remember her purpose, stay focused and keep the sexy man beside her at arm's length when they were alone. Hopefully it wasn't obvious to Aidan that the kiss had such a lasting effect on her.

Apparently, he'd finished protesting the change in their cover story. When they landed at the Sea-Tac Airport, he held her hand on the way to baggage claim and through the rental car line. Once they were on their way, even the new-car smell wasn't enough to distract her from Aidan's crisp, masculine scent. It seemed that one kiss had her locked in on him. She had to shake off this persistent feminine awareness of him. She couldn't allow anything to splinter her focus.

Knowing the city better than he did, she had offered to drive. Seattle was always bustling, and for the first time she was grateful for the snarl of traffic. It gave her more time to consider her approach. She tapped her fingers against the steering wheel while her mind surged into overdrive. She found her eagerness for the confrontation with her mother had faded, knowing she'd have a witness as cool and calm as Aidan.

"What about the ring?"

His question cut into her thoughts and she struggled to find the context. "Ring?" Frankie glanced at him. "What are you talking about?"

"If we're engaged, you should have a ring."

"That doesn't matter. Lots of engaged women go without a ring." She couldn't think of an example right now, but it had to be true. No way would she let him put a ring on her finger. "My mom's a romantic. She'll believe us if we tell her we were planning to shop for a ring together."

"I don't know."

"Trust me."

Aidan turned a bit in the seat, facing her. "I don't know you well enough to trust you."

That stung a little. "You have my file and we can cover the basics tonight," she protested. Why couldn't that be enough? She didn't need him cluttering the plan. "Just gloss over the details, get mushy once in a while when she's watching, and it will work out. We aren't going to be here that long."

"Uh-huh." His gaze returned to the congested roadway. "Why would I propose without a ring? I don't think that's something you'd tolerate."

"You just said you didn't know me."

"I said I didn't trust you. As for knowing you, I'm a quick study," he stated.

"Are you messing with me?" The freeway was at a full stop, so she gave him a long, hard look. The grin creased his face, ornery as hell and way too sexy. *Eyes on the road*, she ordered herself. "I don't wear jewelry."

"You're wearing earrings."

She thought of the small diamond studs in her ears. They'd been a gift from her father on her sixteenth birthday. She touched her ear with a fingertip, giving the simple, timeless setting a twirl. "These hardly count. I wore them to remind my navy buddies I was a girl."

"I have a hard time believing they'd forget that detail."

Frankie ignored what sounded like a compliment, her mind returning to the bigger problem of how best to greet her mom tomorrow.

Smiling would be the toughest part of this farce. Frankie had to find a way. A happy smile and sticking close enough to the truth that her mother wouldn't pinpoint the lies right away was the key to operational success. Oh, how the mighty had fallen. It hadn't been so long ago that the keys to a successful operation were preparation, attitude and the right equipment.

"We need to stop at a mall or something," Aidan said.

Frankie knew she needed better wardrobe options, but shopping was the last thing she wanted to add to their task list. "What did you forget?"

"Not for me, for your mom. It's rude to show up on someone's doorstep empty-handed," he said. "As your fiancé I should bring flowers to the first meeting."

She sighed, frustrated with his sudden commitment to her idea. "You're overthinking it." One of them had to keep this charade under control. "We'll grab a bouquet from a grocery store in the morning."

"I know you're angry with her, but I have standards. Flowers are friendly, polite and thoughtful."

"You didn't toss out this many objections on the plane," she said.

"I was processing the idea and we were in public."

"Right." She wasn't falling for that line. "You're an investigator. You process in real time."

"Not always. Indulge me and stop at the mall. I only need fifteen minutes."

"She doesn't need mall flowers."

"A future son-in-law showing up with cheap flowers is worse than no flowers. I can make you stop."

Frankie would like to see him try. "Would you just drop this, please?"

"No. This was your idea," he said. "Unless you'd rather go back to the original plan?"

"No." Catching on, she bit back the rant. She recognized a test when it smacked her in the face. Aidan had agreed to play this her way, and she wasn't letting him off the hook just because he was trying to annoy her. "We'll stop at the mall."

"I've found a couple of florists close to your house."

"Sophia's house," she corrected. The last

family home Frankie knew had been the general's residence on the post. Sophia had moved quickly after the funeral to the more fashionable Queen Anne neighborhood. "I was an army brat. We moved to a new post every few years. And we're off topic again," she said through gritted teeth. "I'm at home in Savannah now." Sophia's address had stopped feeling like home when her father died.

Aidan mentioned two addresses and names of florist shops. "Which one is better?"

"I have no idea," Frankie said. "Just pick one."

He did and his phone started rattling off the directions for the altered route.

Following the prompts, they reached a sprawling shopping center less than an hour later. After parking in front of the flower shop, they got out of the car. As Frankie reached for the florist's door, she realized Aidan was headed to another store, two doors down. "This way," she called after him.

"We'll get there. Come here for a second."

What was he up to? She glanced at the hours posted on the door. "They close in half an hour."

"Then hurry," he said.

The sly expression on his handsome face challenged her and his quiet voice carried a clear command. Doing nothing to hide her irritation, she stalked over and realized he'd stopped in front of a jewelry store. "No." She crossed her arms. She was *not* going inside.

He leaned down and kissed her. That quick, brief kiss was enough to turn her knees to jelly.

"Yes," he countered. "We're going to do this right to be sure our cover holds up."

"You can't be serious." He couldn't possibly mean to buy her an engagement ring.

"I'm not a man who does things halfway," he said. "Your mother will pick up on that and wonder why I rushed to propose before I was prepared."

"This is *pretend*," Frankie whispered through gritted teeth.

"But it's supposed to look *real*," he retorted with an exasperating laugh. "When I propose to the right woman, I'll have a ring. We can't have Sophia thinking I'm flighty or unreliable. We want the woman to hire me, right?"

Frankie shook her head, wishing for a hole to open up and swallow her. It would solve so many problems. Her back was stiff, her legs aching from the flight. She needed to get to the hotel so she could stretch out the kinks. Seeing her mother while dealing with the undercurrent of pain would be a disadvantage. She'd already lost the element of surprise when Victoria insisted on that phone call. Frankie wouldn't give up more ground. "Fine." Better to give in and get back on track. "Solitaire, classic setting, no bells, whistles or wedding bands."

"Deal." He opened the door for her.

She didn't care for the amusement glinting in his deep blue eyes. "Are you charging it as a work expense?"

"Of course not," he replied, clearly offended.

She let him take her hand as they walked to the glass counter full of engagement settings. Her heart kicked against her rib cage and a familiar spike of pain shot down her leg. She pulled in a slow, deep breath to help unlock her seizing muscles, which were straining against the hardware that kept her pinned together. Frankie forced herself to match his longer stride, refusing to trip or lean on him. Sheer willpower carried her closer to the twinkling gems on display, when she wanted to be anywhere else.

She felt a trickle of sweat at the nape of her neck, under her hair. Aidan might have imagined proposing to a woman, but it wasn't a milestone Frankie had ever given much thought to. Her career had been at the forefront of her mind, and working in close quarters with men took a lot of the shine off the idea of choosing one man for a lifetime. Casual dates and having a good time with friends were enough for her, especially after watching her parents' relationship disintegrate. It would be a long time before commitment and permanence broke the top ten of her priority list.

While the injury had sent her career in a new direction, it had only emphasized the lack of potential for her personal life. At one time, Frankie had wanted that devoted partnership her parents had shared. Now that idyllic romance was clouded by secrets, lies and questions that might never get answered.

The last place she belonged was here, admiring the glitter and responsibility of diamond engagement rings. "You know what?" She patted Aidan's hand. "I'd like to be surprised, after all. You know what I like." She forced her lips into a bright smile. It felt as if her face would crack from the effort. "I know what kind of bouquet will win Mom over. I'll get the flowers while you handle this."

"That's a great idea, sweetheart," Aidan said smoothly. "Let's just get you sized first." His smile looked completely natural when he greeted the salesman. "I meet the future in-laws at brunch tomorrow," he said. "Can't leave any room for doubts or bad first impressions."

"You've landed a smart man," the salesman said.

Frankie swallowed and managed a shaky nod. The metal sizing rings jangled as the salesman slid one loop after another over the fourth finger of her left hand. Her stomach cramped. If she didn't get out of here soon, it was going to get ugly.

The salesman noted her ring size and she walked away as swiftly as possible without breaking into a sprint. A ring made all this too real, too extravagant. How did she keep getting outmaneuvered?

When they were done here, they were going to have a conversation about the ground rules going forward. No more games. No more kisses. This was her problem and she was going to regain control of the operation.

AIDAN WATCHED HER LEAVE. More than a little concerned she'd take the car and leave him stranded, he'd palmed the key while she was struggling with whatever was going on behind those big brown eyes.

He'd been sure the idea of a ring would be enough to call her bluff on this engagement idea. Well, he'd just consider this practice, he decided, pointing out a few settings that he liked.

"She claims to want simple and classic," he explained to Ted, the salesman. Aidan answered questions about his budget and barely refrained from inquiring about the return policy. If her mother had the connections and skills Frankie and Victoria implied, she could send someone out to pester Ted about this sale. Aidan didn't want to give Frankie any reason to say this engagement nonsense had failed because of him.

She'd said no bells and whistles, and no wedding bands—obviously—but he didn't take the first glittering gem Ted showed him. Once he'd examined his favorites, he chose a three-quarter-carat princess cut on a flared band of white gold. It made the best statement. Classic, clean lines. The white gold matched the setting of her earrings. The stone was big enough without overpowering her slender, fine-boned hand.

He'd just completed the purchase and was waiting for the jeweler to adjust the sizing when the door chimed and Frankie returned, carrying an arrangement of some sort wrapped in tissue paper. The sweet fragrance filled the store. "They tell me these will pop and stay beautiful for days," she said, leaving as much distance as possible between the two of them.

He tried to decipher the scent to avoid sympathizing with her obvious discomfort. "Roses?"

"No." She shook her head, her nose wrinkling. "Lilies and tulips. Her favorites. She'll be wrapped around your finger in an instant."

"That's helpful," he said, rocking back on his

heels. "Ted tells me your ring will be sized and polished shortly."

"Great." Her smile was brittle. "I'll, um, put these in the car."

"It can wait." Aidan stepped forward, crowding her just a bit. "I missed you." He brushed his lips to the corner of her mouth. "Did you miss me?"

She wanted to snarl at him, that was clear, but he was only playing the part that matched her idea. He needed her to go all in or bail out before they showed up on her mother's doorstep.

"I hardly know what to do with myself without you," she said, her voice far too sweet.

He laughed and took the flowers from her hands, setting the vase near the register. "Are you hungry?"

She shook her head again.

Aidan suspected pain and nerves were blocking her appetite. The faint brackets around her lush mouth and her stiff posture clued him in. If he thought she'd open up, he'd ask more questions about her recovery. She hid her injury well and he believed she was close to 100 percent. That didn't mean he couldn't be thoughtful or help her manage what must be challenging at times. He just had to do it in a way that didn't offend her.

Ted caught their attention as he returned with

a small, emerald-colored velvet box. "All set," he said, handing it to Aidan.

For such a tiny thing, it felt damned heavy in his hand. He studied Frankie's face as he popped open the lid, giving her a glimpse inside. "Will that do?"

Her eyes were huge as she looked at the ring, then up at him. "Aidan..."

He waited, but she didn't finish. "I think we hit the mark, Ted. Thanks." His fingers felt thick and sluggish as he pulled out the ring and nudged it gently onto Frankie's finger.

His breath backed up in his throat and he felt light-headed. Getting sick here would ruin the moment and he willed his stomach to stop churning. He'd vowed never to go through these motions again. Knowing it wasn't real didn't seem to help matters. He blinked away the hazy memories until he saw Frankie's hand, the new ring and nothing more.

She flared her fingers, her gaze locked on the ring, her lips parted in surprise. "Aidan, I... It looks so—"

He kissed her before she could finish and blow their cover. "I'm honored you said yes." He handed her the flowers and guided her quickly from the store.

At the car, he opened the passenger door for her. "I'll drive. You look a little shell-shocked."

He closed the door before she could answer, but the silence didn't last.

"What are you thinking?" she exclaimed as he backed out of the parking space.

"If it's too small, speak now and I'll exchange it," he said, his voice rough with the emotions he couldn't quite block out.

She swore. "You know it isn't. This is crazy, Aidan."

"Your idea or my cooperation?" What did he have to do to get her to drop this?

"Be serious," she snapped. "You can't just buy me a ring." She started to tug it off. "Go back to the store."

He pulled into the next available parking space. "Have you changed your mind about this approach?"

She glared at him, her hands tangled in her lap, the vase of flowers sitting at her feet. "No."

"Then it stays on." The command came out with more heat than he'd intended. "Think of it as the prop that will reinforce the story you want your mother to believe."

"You don't get a prop from a real jeweler."

"That's a matter of opinion." He set the navigation on his cell phone for the hotel they'd booked. "I suggest you get used to it. If your mother or anyone else catches you without it, you'll have bigger lies to weave." His second engagement was going far worse than the first one. At least this time around he knew it was temporary. Hopefully when he met her mother he'd have a better understanding of why Frankie insisted on this tactic.

"Fine." She drummed her palms on her knees. "It's just—"

"Find a complimentary word," he warned.

Aidan shook off the frustration and bad memories as they merged with the traffic. As the silence stretched he figured she couldn't find a compliment, or she was plotting her next strategic maneuver. Either way, he was grateful for the momentary truce. When he'd pulled to a stop under the hotel awning, he turned to her again. "Did you think to change our reservation to a single room?"

She sagged back into the seat. "No." She reached across the console, her hand soft on his arm, the diamond bright on her finger. "But let me handle this one, okay?"

Unsure whether that was wise, he brainstormed ways to mitigate the damage if she launched yet another surprise attack or kept the separate rooms.

Instinctively taking in the surroundings, Aidan logged every face and position of the other guests in the lobby. He'd reviewed everything Victoria had sent him last night when he was battling the typical new-case insomnia.

Sophia Leone co-owned a security company after her years as an analyst for the alphabet soup in Washington, DC. Her own daughter suspected her of abusing her position to eliminate her husband. To support the case, the Colby Agency hadn't bothered to hide their travel itinerary, and Frankie had told her mother she'd be arriving today. As the widow of a high-powered general, Sophia must have a vast network of friends from all over the globe. Aidan knew he and Frankie would be at a disadvantage in these early hours. It wasn't paranoia to suspect someone was on-site keeping watch.

Which guest was here as a favor to Sophia? Which one would report Frankie had arrived with a man acting like a boyfriend? Aidan put a mental tag on the two most likely candidates and then shifted most of his attention to Frankie as she checked in.

He was glad they planned to keep the initial mother-daughter reunion brief, so they'd have time to review the key players at Leo Solutions tonight. With any luck, his contact at Interpol would have more information on the passports Frankie had found.

"Adjoining rooms?" Frankie queried. "I was sure I booked a suite." She bumped Aidan's shoulder as she pulled out her phone. "How did I mix that up? Honey, do you have the confirmation I emailed you?"

Aidan pulled his phone from his pocket. "Let me take a look."

"We'll get it straightened out," the woman at the desk assured her.

"We just got engaged," Frankie explained, letting the diamond flash. "We're here to surprise the family." Her smile was as bright as the diamond. "I'm so excited." She rubbed her hand up and down his arm. "I probably clicked the wrong box by mistake."

Impressed—affected—by her performance, he cursed himself for asking her to commit to the role of excited fiancée. He should've just said no to the cover story change. She thought he was worried about her physically, when her emotional state concerned him more. Now he feared he'd fall for her if they kept this up. What a fool he was.

"Congratulations." The woman checking them in admired the ring before setting her fingers on the keyboard. "I do have a suite available. Let me just…" She tapped more keys. "That should do it." She glanced up and beamed at them. "I've adjusted the rate through the weekend." She programmed two key cards and tucked them into a small envelope, pushing it across the counter. With a map of the hotel, she pointed out their room and the basic amenities. "You'll be right here with an excellent view of the city," she said, circling what appeared to be a corner room. "Park wherever you like. The closest elevators are down the first corridor on your left." She pointed. "Do you need help with your luggage?"

"I'll manage," Aidan said. He wanted some privacy, and fast. He didn't want Frankie second-guessing or throwing him another curveball.

They made it up to the suite in one trip even with the flowers. Frankie walked inside and stopped short in the center of the room. "Holy cow. That view. We should get engaged more often."

The "we" gave him pause, though she was right to be thinking in teamwork terms. He blamed the strange twitch between his shoulder blades on the residual effect of sliding that ring onto her finger. Stepping up beside her, he enjoyed the floor-to-ceiling corner window that gave them a panoramic view of Seattle's west side. "You have a beautiful hometown."

"That's overstating it."

Her reflexive disagreement made him feel better somehow. "Did you ever live in a place that felt like a hometown?"

She turned away from the windows to set the vase of wrapped flowers on the tall dresser next to the television. "We moved a lot, obviously. Wherever we lived, there were certain items that went in specific places. Little things like the key rack near the door, a family portrait in the dining room. My mom's theory was those details made the transitions easier."

He followed as she rolled her suitcase into the bedroom. "Did it work?"

She looked over her shoulder, a mix of nostalgia and sorrow clouding her eyes. "Yes."

Should he point out the mixed messages she gave him about her mother? It was as if she described two different women: one a devoted wife and mother, possibly a hopeless romantic, and the other a sharp mind capable of wreaking havoc on the world at large.

A fresh awareness, and a desperate ache to fix everything for Frankie, filled him. Had he learned nothing from his mistakes? He was an investigator, end of story. He had to remember that, had to keep his focus on the facts, for her safety and his.

He backed toward the door. "I'm going to check on the leads I was working on those passports."

"Fine," she said, not looking at him. "I'll, um, work out a few things in here."

"Is an hour enough time?"

The only sign of tension was the little catch in her breathing. "That works for me."

## Chapter Six

Frankie let Aidan drive to her mother's new house in Queen Anne while she held the flowers. Periodically she stretched her hands to relieve the tension that mounted with every passing block. After some restorative yoga in the hotel room, she felt better, stronger and ready to calmly face whatever came next. Though it hadn't done any good last time, a tiny part of her still wanted to charge in and blast her mother with an all-out attack.

Unfortunately, unless she used the condemning statement Sophia had signed, Frankie didn't have anything else confirmed enough to ask about. Aidan hadn't turned up any concrete information on the passports. The best he could tell, they'd never been used, despite the stamps inside. So why had they been in the safe-deposit box? Frankie reminded herself things were moving forward, intelligently if not quickly. For the first time since getting kicked out of the navy, she didn't feel alone.

She slid a glance at her undercover groom as they neared her mother's home, wondering what kind of reception to expect. Would it be stilted and weird or warm and happy? Her last conversation with her mom, in the cemetery at her father's grave, had been tense and ugly. Grief-stricken, she'd tossed out accusations and hammered Sophia with questions she wouldn't answer. Frankie prepared for an awkward encounter, though Sophia would surely pour on the charm with Aidan around.

Sunlight caught on the engagement ring. The fragrant scent of lilies filled the car. Frankie was showing up at her mother's house with a fiancé and a bouquet of flowers. Her emotions swung from one extreme to the other with every heartbeat as Aidan pulled to a stop in front of the house. The struggle had her waffling between the idea that going to Victoria had been smart, and the possibility that it had been foolish. Frankie needed investigative support to get justice and clear her father's name. No, she needed only one honest answer. It reminded her of being caught in an undertow. She could see the sunlight, knew where she needed to go, while an unseen force dragged her out to sea.

She looked up at the tidy Craftsman house

with trimmed hedges lining the walkway and steps up to the porch, which was framed with flower boxes on the railing. The ironwork table and chairs had decorated patios or porches in various homes where they'd lived around the world for as long as Frankie could remember. How many quiet moments had her parents shared at that table over the years? What did it mean that her mother still had those pieces?

"This makes no sense."

"Which part?" Aidan studied her closely. "Your mom hasn't seen the ring or me. There's still time for the original game plan."

"The engagement is the only piece of this puzzle I trust to work as expected." Frankie stared at the table and chairs.

"Is that an attempt to scare me off?"

"No." Her heavy sigh rippled across the tissue covering the flowers. She pushed the bouquet into his hands. "We're on, my darling fiancé. Let's make it count."

They climbed out of the car and Aidan locked the doors with the key fob. "Play nice," he murmured, brushing a kiss to her cheek as they walked up to the porch. "I've got your back."

She wanted to roll her eyes. He had no idea what he was walking into, though she was ridiculously grateful he was with her.

Her mother must've been watching from a

window. The front door flew open the moment they topped the stairs. Sophia hovered in the doorway, her hands clutched over her heart.

"Frankie," she breathed. "Oh, thank heaven. You're home." She drew her into a crushing hug.

Frankie patted her mother's shoulders, biting back the snide observation that a house she'd never seen couldn't be home. There would be time for barbs like that later. Indulging her petty streak now would undermine the ultimate goal: to get the truth out of Sophia.

"Mom," Frankie said, escaping the embrace. "This is Aidan Abbot."

Aidan extended the vase of flowers. "It's a pleasure to meet you, Ms. Leone."

Sophia's eyes, shining with unshed tears, darted from Frankie to Aidan and back again. "Come in, come in. Any friend of Frankie's—"

"Fiancé," Frankie clarified. "We started as friends, though." She imagined whoever she married—if she married—would have to be a friend first. She held up her hand to show off the ring and sell the lie. Sophia's eyes widened and her lips parted, but she couldn't seem to speak. When they got back to the hotel, Frankie would admit to Aidan that he had been right about the ring making all the difference.

"Oh, come in! Come in here and tell me everything." Sophia gripped Frankie's hand for a closer inspection. Looking to Aidan, she said, "You have excellent taste."

"I thought it suited her." A smug grin crossed his face as they followed Sophia inside. "Frankie wouldn't have taken my proposal seriously without it."

Sophia beamed at her. "That's my girl," she said with pride.

Clearly Aidan planned to gloat over this when they were alone. At least Frankie could revel in being right about her mother's mushy romantic side. Thoughts of who'd trumped whom faded as her eyes landed on the family portrait hanging in a place of honor over the sideboard in the dining room. She stopped short, staring.

Sophia paused, as well. "You seem surprised," she said after a moment.

"Look at you." Aidan gave her hand a squeeze as he admired the portrait. "You're so happy."

Frankie would argue as soon as she got over the shock. Had Sophia put this here when she'd moved in, or had she dug it out of storage just for the visit today?

"That was painted when we were in Germany," Sophia explained to Aidan. "Frankie was seven. The local artist worked from a snapshot…"

Frankie stopped listening. Her mind had traveled back to those idyllic days when everything in her world had made sense. Her father had been a respected leader, her mother outgoing and friendly and involved with the community. Frankie had had a normal life and her body had cooperated every day. She hadn't known what real deception was, had no concept of scandal. Granted, she'd been seven and generally oblivious of anything beyond school and her young friends.

"You and Dad went to Austria for your anniversary that year," she said wistfully.

"That's right." Sophia cleared her throat. "How do you remember that?"

"I got to have a sleepover with Elise Stafford while you were gone."

"You two were always getting into trouble."

"That sounds like a story I need to hear," Aidan said, raising Frankie's hand to his lips and kissing her knuckles. "Who's going to tell me?"

Frankie let her mother do the honors. She was too busy analyzing why the pieces and collections they'd gathered to maintain that sense of home were displayed here.

She'd expected a woman capable of throwing her husband to the wolves would have purged all the reminders or shipped them to her daughter. It wasn't as if Frankie had given her time to prepare for the visit, either. Hardly twenty-four hours had passed since she reached out from Victoria Colby's office.

Sophia, relaxed and in her element as hostess, offered them water or lemonade and shared a few of Frankie's childhood highlights with Aidan as if there'd never been any strife between them. Frankie wanted to snap and claw; she wanted to demand the truth. The words nearly tumbled free—*to hell with patience, charades, proper channels and procedures*. She had only one question: *Hey, Mom, why'd you set up Dad?*

Except it would backfire. Her mother's stoic mask would slam into place and they'd be no closer to the source of information Frankie was sure they'd find somewhere inside Leo Solutions. Better to follow her mother's example, appearing to be one thing while carrying on as something else entirely in the shadows.

"Frankie?" Aidan bumped her knee with his.

"Pardon?" She forced her lips into a smile.

"Your mom asked about your back," he said, giving her hand another squeeze.

"Oh. It's fine." She hurried to elaborate when Sophia's face fell. "I'm running again."

"Oh, Frankie, that's wonderful. I know that was an important goal."

Her mother knew damn good and well the most important goal had been resuming active duty with the navy. Frankie smiled through the stinging bitterness of failure. "It feels good," she said, playing nice. "I'll be able to dance at my wedding, too." Though her father wouldn't be there to walk her down the aisle, she added silently.

"I can't wait!" Sophia leaned forward. "Tell me how you met."

Here came another undertow. Frankie gripped Aidan's hand in both of hers, hoping he'd get the hint and dive in. They'd come up with a loose cover story, but she couldn't seem to get it started.

"We met on a case she was working for the Savannah PD," he began. The way he told the story, she could see it in her mind. He made it sound as though he found her interesting and likable. Quite a feat, since she'd forced him into this engagement ruse. The man was excellent undercover and she owed him big for this. By the time he finished, she almost believed how much they loved each other, right down to an all-too-real startling rush of affection for him that soothed her nerves.

"Your daughter amazes me at every turn," Aidan said, raising their joined hands to his lips once more. "I can't tell you how happy I am that she agreed to marry me."

"This is wonderful," Sophia gushed, right on cue. "What do you have in mind so far?"

"In mind?" Frankie jerked her gaze from Aidan to her mother.

"For the wedding." Sophia laced her fingers together, bouncing a little in her seat. "We need to start planning."

A bear trap locked around her ankle would be more comfortable. "I, um…" Frankie cleared the tight ball of dread out of her throat. Her mother was supposed to be enchanted by the romance, distracted by a future son-in-law. She was supposed to respect Frankie's space, not swoop in with talk of wedding plans. "I'm still adjusting to being engaged. The rest can wait."

For the right guy and preferably for a time when she wasn't consumed with clearing her father's name.

"We wanted to tell you first," Aidan added smoothly.

Sophia's delighted smile only grew brighter with every word Aidan uttered. "How did your parents react?"

"Well, they're in Ireland," Aidan explained. "They sounded happy enough when I called."

Sophia's smile retreated as concern filled her eyes. "You haven't met them?"

"Not yet," Frankie said, improvising. She hadn't considered this wrinkle. "I look forward to it." She glanced at Aidan, deciding his family must be wonderful based on him: smart and confident and wrapped in that sexy chiseled exterior.

Chiseled? Good grief, the game she'd started was fooling her. She tugged her hand free of his and pushed herself to her feet. Pretending to be relaxed and in love was making her jittery.

"Are you okay? Can I get you something?"

"I'm fine, Mom," she said too quickly. "It was just a long flight." *Play nice. Stay calm.* She walked toward the kitchen island and refilled her glass from the water pitcher Sophia had set out. "I tried to nap, but the hotel mattress was lumpy."

"The girl could star in a modern *Princess and the Pea*," Sophia told Aidan.

"I've noticed she likes things a certain way." His eyes gleamed with amusement. "And I like making her happy."

"We doted on her," Sophia admitted. "Siblings might have helped, but it never worked out."

"What?" This was the first Frankie had ever heard about siblings. "You tried to have more kids?"

"There's no need to be offended now," her mother said with a sad smile. "Your father and I wanted a big family and we had high hopes, considering how quickly I got pregnant with you. But I never carried another baby past twelve weeks."

How could the woman blurt out a personal confession in front of a stranger and yet not be honest with her own daughter about her husband's trial and suicide? Frankie shot Aidan a helpless glance. "I never knew."

"It doesn't matter to me." His kind smile loosened the knot twisting in her gut. Whoever he eventually married would be a lucky woman, on the receiving end of that kind of attention. "Our future is sure to have plenty of ups and downs."

Truer words, she thought, her head still spinning with Sophia's latest revelation. Maybe she suspected Frankie's motives for showing up now, and this was her own form of diversion.

"By the time you were old enough to understand, we'd stopped trying." Sophia was everything calm and open. "It was something I meant to discuss with you woman to woman, but we never found the time."

"I get it." Frankie gulped her water. "Aidan's right." She couldn't meet his gaze. "I'm sure we'll have plenty of issues to work through along our way."

"You're ahead of the game knowing that's part of married life," Sophia agreed. "The doctors never suggested it was hereditary."

First wedding talk and now kids? Frankie wanted the world to slow down so she could step off for a few minutes. It was too domestic and too strange, considering their last conversation and the resulting estrangement. "We'll cross that bridge when we get there, Mom." She would *not* discuss reproduction in front of Aidan.

"Of course." Sophia came to the counter and refilled her water glass, as well. "Why don't you two check out of the hotel and move in here?"

Frankie choked, coughed. "No. No, thanks." She couldn't play the adoring fiancée role 24/7. "Mom, really, we're fine at the hotel."

"I understand." Sophia made an examination of the ice in her glass. "How long will you be in town?"

Crap, Frankie was blowing the happy-daughter-here-for-a-fresh-start routine.

"That depends." Aidan stepped up, his warm smile the epitome of devoted groom as he smoothed over her gaffe. "Since I met your daughter, it's been clear how important family is to her. One reason we haven't given the wedding much thought is that she wants to share that process with you."

"Is that true?"

Frankie could only nod at the impending train wreck.

"I'm not one to waste time," Aidan continued. "I lit a fire of sorts under my future bride. I sent résumés to several companies, including Leo Solutions, in hopes of landing a job right away."

When he wrapped his arm around Frankie's shoulders, it felt so...normal.

"Frankie took leave from the Savannah PD," he went on, "so we could spend some time out here and see how it goes."

"Then you *must* stay here," Sophia insisted. "There's plenty of room. I'll find places for you both within the company. Think of it as a test drive. No obligation." She hesitated, hope shining in her eyes. "Or if you find the work suits you, we can make it permanent. It's what your father and I wanted all along."

"Mom." Just the mention of her father set her teeth on edge. "Your home—"

"Will always have room for you."

"Thank you, Sophia." Aidan stepped into the breach once more. "That's generous and we appreciate it, of course."

Frankie rubbed the scar her mother knew about on her hip, the one still shedding bits of dirt from that wretched road. "I keep weird hours with the physical therapy and early-morning workouts. Besides, we're used to being alone."

Sophia's cheeks turned pink. "I do understand. Why don't we get you set up in a corporate apartment? At least until you decide if you're staying."

Frankie was about to turn that down, too, when she heard Aidan accepting it with enthusiasm. "A corporate apartment? That's not an imposition?"

"Not at all. I'm happy to do it. They're fully furnished, have a scheduled housekeeping service and provide great access to markets and entertainment downtown. The interns love the location."

"Great. Thanks." Frankie almost meant it.

Sophia glanced at her watch. "I'm supposed to check in at the office to review a client proposal before dinner. Why don't we all head over? You can meet my business partner, Paul Sterling, and we can discuss possible posts for each of you."

Frankie couldn't get out of the house fast enough. She didn't try to convince herself it was all about the case and getting a look inside Leo Solutions. If her mother had been so determined to eliminate her dad, why did she keep so many reminders of the life they'd shared? The contradiction seemed like an unsolvable puzzle.

Or it would have if she'd been here alone. Few things seemed impossible as she walked hand in hand with the man pretending to be in love with her. The realization didn't make her particularly happy, but that analysis would have to wait for another day.

"YOUR MOM SEEMS genuinely happy to see you again," Aidan said, sliding into the driver's seat. He knew the opposite was true for Frankie and he wanted to give her space to vent whatever she was feeling, before round two.

Her lips thinned. "It would be nice if I could take anything she says at face value."

Aidan appreciated her quiet insistence that they follow her mother to the Leo Solutions headquarters rather than riding with her. Frankie had held up like a champ, sticking with the safe topics, but she clearly needed a breather. "How are you doing?" He ignored the way her hands fisted in her lap.

"I'm fine. Thanks to your quick thinking. You're amazing at the undercover routine."

The unexpected compliment sounded sincere. "Thanks. It got a little dicey here and there."

"Did the wedding talk upset you?"

*Yes.* "Not too bad." Talk of kids had been worse. He concentrated on relaxing his grip on the steering wheel. A year ago fatherhood had been one of those murky, inevitable points in his future. Now he'd written it off as something he wasn't qualified to think about. "You made it sound as though she'd ask for DNA and blood samples."

"She might yet," Frankie replied, her gaze firmly on Sophia's car ahead of them. "It's probably part of the new-hire process."

"Well, I think we're doing great."

"You can't be sure," she countered.

"I am sure. You were right about the engagement tactic." Her ego needed a boost and her mind needed the distraction. "She's in love with the idea of you being in love." He waited, surprised when Frankie didn't give him an I-told-you-so. "I saw the way you sized up her place. Planning to break in?"

"No," she said, her brief laugh tinged with exhaustion. "I was just startled by how many things sitting around were from our previous homes." She scowled.

"You weren't thinking about floor safes and security systems?"

"Only a little." She twisted the diamond ring on her finger. "Do you think she did the painting and other stuff just to impress me?"

"I doubt it." He wasn't sure Frankie wanted his opinion right now. From his vantage point, Sophia was fully devoted to repairing her relationship with her daughter.

"Nice work buying your way in to a highly

competitive job for the small investment of an engagement ring."

"Small investment?" He faked indignation. "I would've gotten the job, anyway. Interviewers love me." Though he was teasing, he felt her focus on him and he struggled not to fidget under that steady examination.

"I bet they do," she said. "The flowers were a nice touch."

Another compliment. It gave him hope for surviving the situation. "It pleases me that you're pleased." He flashed her a grin.

She gave him one of those scoffing snorts. "Do you think her partner, Paul, will start us in the mail room?"

"She's surely discussing the options with him already. She's been on the phone since she pulled out of the driveway."

"I noticed." Frankie's hands tensed up again. "What sort of position does she think you're qualified for?"

"I can hardly say. I'm former Interpol. The agency loaded my résumé with fitness and combat training expertise. Self-defense, hand-to-hand, various firearms."

"Nice."

He felt his chest swell that she was impressed. "And you?"

"At the end of the day, I'm an analyst like my mom."

She didn't sound happy about the comparison. "You're far more than that," he said automatically.

Frankie shrugged one shoulder. "She could fit me in as a trainer, but she won't. I don't think she'll ever let go of how weak I was right after those early surgeries."

*Surgeries, plural?* He wanted her to volunteer more information about her injury and recovery so he could avoid an invasion of her medical privacy. "You look perfectly fit to me."

"Is that a sincere compliment?" She was staring at him again.

"Yes." He shot her a smile. "Did you think the things I said in front of your mother weren't sincere?"

"No other conclusion." Frankie didn't sound the least perturbed. "You don't know me."

Every word he'd said in front of her mom, he believed. Unfortunately, he couldn't give Frankie an answer she'd accept, so he changed the subject. "What do you know about Paul Sterling?"

"Only what we looked at last night." She shifted in the seat. "Did you get the impression there's a personal connection?"

"I hope not." Anything personal between Paul

and Sophia threw a wrench into his assessment of the investigation. Bad enough he might have to anticipate how Sophia would rank her relationship with her daughter amid her commitments to the company. A lover only increased the twists exponentially, not to mention how Frankie would react. The last thing she needed was more pain. "We'll know soon enough," he said, taking the last turn into an industrial park near the airport.

They followed Sophia past the security guard at the gate and parked in a space behind the one reserved with her name on it. He caught Frankie's hand before she could get out of the car. "You're doing great," he said, his gaze locked with hers. "And you're not alone."

She shocked him with a quick kiss on his lips and a hot smile. "Game on."

Knowing this was all show for her mother, Aidan felt frustrated that his immediate reaction had nothing to do with the case. The kick in his pulse, the flash of heat under his skin were all about the woman. He watched her stride up to join her mom and wondered if his attraction was as one-sided as it felt.

"Paul's waiting for us in my office," Sophia announced.

Another warning that the man's purpose went beyond business.

Like Frankie, Aidan was cataloging every detail as they walked into the lobby. The information placard showed Leo Solutions had offices listed on the top two floors and one lower level of the seven-story building, with other companies scattered in between. The place was quiet, the furnishings expensive and understated. A tall vase exploding with fresh flowers spanned the space between the banks of elevators. He imagined clients felt safe and reassured doing business here.

"Do you always work on Saturdays?" he asked, when the three of them stepped into an elevator.

"Not always," Sophia replied. "We have a new client we're courting." Her eyes sparkled as her gaze danced between the two of them.

Aidan took Frankie's hand in his, a casual gesture of affection that Sophia noticed.

"Paul pulled your résumé, Aidan. I know some people might see it as favoritism, but I'm glad you told me you'd applied." She held the door open when they reached her floor. "Welcome to Leo Solutions."

Frankie's fingers tightened around his hand. He gave them a reassuring squeeze.

"We have offices on this floor and the next floor up. And a fully equipped gym and training space on the first sublevel."

"Is there anywhere in Seattle that doesn't have a great view?" Aidan asked as they strolled by a bank of windows.

"The views, the weather and the recreational variety were the things we enjoyed most as a family. Right, Frankie?"

"I remember."

"I just couldn't see planting the business anywhere else. Your father and I even looked at this building together."

"Really?"

"Really." Sophia's reply was a whispered echo, her gaze locked on the view beyond the wide windows running the length of the far wall. "Let's not keep Paul waiting. He's eager to meet you both."

Aidan hoped she wasn't putting words into her business partner's mouth. He hadn't been able to get through the company finances or the partnership agreement, so he didn't know if Paul would see Frankie as a threat or an asset. Although Sophia's warm welcome gave him the impression Frankie, as her only family, would be a beneficiary at the very least, it was too soon to know for sure.

Sophia led them down a hallway framed by cubicles on one side and small offices on the other. Her office suite was preceded by a receptionist's desk and double doors, currently standing open. Paul, seeing them, walked over from the seating area near the corner window. He smiled as Sophia made the introductions, but Aidan didn't feel any warmth in the expression.

"It's good to meet you," Paul said to Frankie as they settled into the seating area. "You mean the world to your mother. She's missed you." He took a seat at one end of a long couch and Sophia sat next to him.

Mentally, Aidan swore. There was a romantic liaison between the business partners. As he and Frankie took the chairs opposite the older couple, he noticed the way she eased her body into hers. That cautious transition from standing to sitting was the only allowance he'd seen her make for her injury. He wasn't about to jeopardize any progress he'd made by mentioning it to her.

"Sophia tells me we need to find positions within Leo Solutions." Paul cocked an eyebrow at Aidan. "For both of you."

"Only if it's convenient," he answered. "I'm happy to look for work elsewhere."

"Nonsense. You'll be family soon." Sophia's sharp gaze slid to her partner. "Aidan has the background and qualities we prefer."

He gave Paul his best easygoing smile. "I don't intend to force my way in."

Paul tapped the closed tablet balanced on the

arm of the couch. "I'd flagged your résumé for an interview before Sophia called."

Aidan pretended to believe him.

"We didn't come out to insert ourselves into your business," Frankie interjected quietly as she reached for Aidan's hand. "I'm sure you know things were rough between Mom and me, but when Aidan proposed, I knew I wanted to tell her in person."

"She's willing to stay, Paul," Sophia said, her voice catching. "You know we could use her skills."

He nodded. "Would you rather work a desk or be in the field? I'm sure Sophia's told you we have three divisions offering cyber security, property security and personal protection solutions."

"A desk," Frankie replied, avoiding her mother's gaze.

Aidan saw the tension fall from Sophia's shoulders. It was such a typical, caring, maternal reaction. If he'd suffered Frankie's injuries, his mother would do the same thing. He'd reviewed the bulk of what Frankie labeled as evidence against her mother and he didn't have enough to verify the documentation as real. Still, he wasn't seeing any of the cold animosity Frankie insisted lurked under Sophia's reserved and polished surface.

"Based on your record with the navy and the Savannah Police Department, we can add you as an analyst."

Aidan listened as intently as Frankie while Paul outlined the details of the position.

"You'd be working closely with me, as well," Sophia added.

Aidan was sure that was a mistake, but Frankie managed a smile. "Sounds good."

"My only concern," Paul continued, holding up a hand, "is your status at the Savannah PD. Your supervisor isn't aware you're job hunting. He believes you're out here on extended leave."

If she was going to falter and blow their cover, this would be the moment. "I told him I needed some personal time," Frankie said. "And I agreed to continue consulting on cases as needed." She looked hard at Sophia. "I wasn't sure how things would go here."

"That's perfectly understandable," her mother said.

"Is it?" Paul countered. "We're in the midst of a major client pitch. I'd like to know the team is focused on that primary goal."

Frankie scooted to the edge of her chair. "I'll call in and give my notice on Monday. I'll do it now if you'd prefer."

Aidan watched as a wealth of information passed, unspoken, between the older couple.

"Frankie and I don't mean to put you in a tough position," he said. "We have other options in the area and we can always just call this a vacation."

"This is *home*." Sophia pressed her lips together. "At least I want it to be." Her tender, pleading gaze moved to Frankie. "Give us six months. Please."

Frankie looked to Paul. "Will that work for you?"

He agreed with a nod. "Now, Aidan." His salt-and-pepper eyebrows dipped low. "We have a vacancy in the training division for our personal security team. You'd be overseeing everything from hand-to-hand combat to weapons proficiency."

"Sounds good."

"You're not afraid of paperwork, are you?"

"Not at all."

"Are you willing to venture into the field occasionally to help with planning and assessment?"

"Of course."

Paul stood and extended his hand. "Then welcome to Leo Solutions. We'll get the paperwork sorted on Monday."

The older man was friendly enough, appearing open and content with the new arrivals. Aidan had yet to pinpoint what bothered him about Sophia's business partner. Polite, not quite slick, Paul seemed to be hiding a cold, hard center. The man ran a security company; suspicions went with the job. Maybe he had painted himself as the protector here, of Sophia and the firm. Considering how and when the business had launched, it made some sense. It would've made more sense if Sophia exhibited any sign of weakness.

Like mother, like daughter, Aidan thought, knowing he'd never dare say so in front of Frankie.

Paul turned toward Sophia. "In the meantime, I'm sure you have plenty of catching up in mind."

"I do." She was as delighted as any adoring mother to have her child home, within arm's reach. "We'll start with a company tour, and then I'll take them over to the apartment," she said, leaning close to kiss Paul's cheek. "I'll be back soon to finish that proposal."

# Chapter Seven

*Sunday, April 10, 12:45 p.m.*

Frankie's gaze moved from her empty suitcase to the nearly empty closet in the bedroom of the corporate apartment leased by Leo Solutions. She was wearing the only dress she'd thought to pack, a last-minute item she'd tossed in. Her half of the closet held two pairs of jeans, an assortment of shirts, one pair of khaki slacks and only two pairs of shoes in addition to her runners.

"Problem?" Aidan paused just behind her. "We can always go shopping or have a friend send you whatever you forgot."

"That's not it." She shoved her suitcase into the closet and closed the door. "I guess we're all moved in."

Her limited wardrobe was the least of her troubles. Currently at the top of her list of problems was the *one* bedroom apartment. They'd had more space—possibly more privacy—at the hotel suite. Aidan had made a valid argument when she tried to back out again: they had to make it look as if they were meeting Sophia halfway.

As they were wrapping up brunch, Sophia had invited them once more to stay at the house. Again Frankie refused. Though she'd appreciated Aidan's diplomatic backup, she wasn't as enamored with his small touches, his chivalrous manners and the occasional chaste kiss.

Sophia, however, was overjoyed with every gesture that affirmed Frankie and Aidan were happy together. Unfortunately, while he played the doting-fiancé role like an expert, she struggled against an urge to skitter away. Or worse, burrow into him.

She had to focus, to stay angry with Sophia, but she was losing her grip on that bitter edge. Sophia had always been vibrant and outgoing, and being drenched in her mother's warmth made something deep inside Frankie long for the way things once were. The life she'd worked toward, dreamed of and enjoyed so fleetingly had been ripped apart and scattered.

Her family would never be the same, and not just because the Leones numbered two now instead of three. Frankie believed her mother bore the blame. She'd come all this way to prove it.

Except they weren't finding anything conclusive. She knew Aidan wasn't working against her, precisely. It just didn't feel as though he was working *with* her. Her mother's passports were bogus and he kept casting doubts over the source of the statement and documentation on the flash drive.

Now they were living together in an apartment that might very well be bugged. They couldn't speak freely and couldn't jam a signal without blowing their cover. They would go to the office each day and come back here. The engagement was working, giving them a reason to be together, yet Frankie felt trapped by her own scheme. She finally understood what he'd said on the plane about lying to each other in public.

"I didn't think this through," she said, just in case the bugs were live. "Six months will be an exercise in restraint." She sneered at the closet. "At least we'll have the company gear for work." Bags of Leo Solutions shirts and workout gear had been lined up on the corner of the furnished sofa when they walked in.

"Why don't we head out and see about stocking the kitchen?" he suggested.

"Great idea." She grabbed her purse, her smallest knife tucked inside. While they were out they'd have a chance to talk freely. Of course, that also gave their opponent time to search the apartment. On missions like this one, Frankie knew every choice came with a calculated risk.

It made her feel marginally better when Aidan planted a wireless camera to catch anyone who might enter the apartment. When they were clear of the building, she caught him watching for a tail, because she was doing it, too. "We're a pair," she said with a short laugh.

"A good pair." He took her hand and drew her close to his side, playing his role to perfection once more.

"You don't have to fawn over me all the time."

He only grinned. "Relax. I know you're not big on public displays of affection."

"I'm affectionate," she argued.

He laughed as they crossed the street. "Sure you are. Just keep following my lead."

His assessment gave her pause. "Do you think my mom suspects we're pretending?" That could put an end to her best chance to know the truth.

"No, she's seeing what we want her to see right now."

"Why do I feel slimy?" The moment the words were out, Frankie regretted them. Aidan tensed, just a subtle flex of muscle in his arm, and she chattered to cover the gaffe. "I know this approach was my idea. I stand by it," she insisted. "You said yourself it's working. She's distracted by wedding brain. We'll be able to get what we came for before she knows what happened."

"At this rate you'll be telling her you're pregnant by Friday," he said, his voice cool.

Frankie considered and dismissed the idea as too soon. "The corporate apartment can work for us, too."

"How? You think the doorman knows something?"

"No." Her patience had stretched thin during brunch, but she couldn't let it snap. Aidan was her only ally. She needed him to see the real Sophia under the social sophistication and perfect-mother image. "We'll uncover the truth."

They walked down the block toward the waterfront, admiring the blend of historic and new architecture spiking up around them. Aidan asked her questions about the city and she answered, trying to decide if this was part of the cover. A pleasant breeze toyed with the hem of her skirt. "Are you pleased or disappointed we don't have a tail?" she asked, getting the conversation back to safe ground.

"Pleased," he replied. "She trusts us. Paul might pose the bigger problem."

"Paul's reserved, that's all." Thinking about Sophia's business partner, Frankie couldn't help making a comparison. "He's the polar opposite of my father. Do you think she went for the quiet and serious type this time on purpose?"

"I think she partnered with the man who gave Leo Solutions the best chance to succeed. He and your parents go way back."

"Don't remind me." Aidan had found the connection last night and pieced together the trail. Frankie had been more than a little alarmed by the discovery. Not to mention the kiss her mother had deposited on the man's cheek.

"She wasn't having an affair, Frankie."

"You sound so sure." She reached back and pressed a point on her back, above her hip. Keeping pace with his longer stride created a good ache as her muscles loosened up.

"I am. I've been systematically working through your mother's history."

They'd divided the searches for the purpose of efficiency and objectivity. Everything Frankie found on Sophia only made her cranky, which stalled the progress. So she dug into the general's last months in Afghanistan while Aidan investigated her mom.

"Are you working present to past?" If so, it left her exposed as he learned of her mother's trips to hospitals and spine injury rehab centers to help Frankie recover. She pushed down the swell of embarrassment. Of all the people involved in this mess, she had the fewest secrets.

"A little of both, actually."

She could tell he had more to say, a new question or accusation about her lousy approach on this case. "Spit it out. I can take it."

He stopped to admire a display in a gallery window, draping his arm around her shoulders. They were just a couple out for a walk on a fine Sunday. Though she wanted to sink into the comfort he offered, it was too risky. She couldn't afford to mirror her mother's mistake and get distracted by Aidan's false romance.

"You realize your mom took hits from all sides, nearly all at once."

Frankie caught her scowling reflection in the glass. She nudged him on down the street. "What do you mean?"

"Charges against the general were filed only a few days after you were injured. He was arrested. You were undergoing surgery."

"And?"

"That's a lot for anyone to handle. You were medicated before the surgery. Sedated for nearly two days after. Do you understand she never left your side?"

Frankie had no memory of the day before the IED or those immediately following. She'd learned the facts from her doctors and the survivors from her team. She had only a hazy recollection of Sophia being nearby in those early days.

"You're implying my mom chose me over my dad."

"I'm not implying. I'm saying it outright."

Frankie glanced around for a distraction, uncomfortable with the way her heart cramped at his words. "Another way might be to say she was already distancing herself from his problems."

Aidan sighed. "You told Victoria you tried to have a civilized conversation with your mom about your father's case."

"A complete disaster," Frankie admitted. People were bustling around them now as they strolled by vendors in Pike Place Market. The produce was bright and the scents of greens and fruits mingled with flowers and seafood and the close waterfront. She knew they'd have to return with something or eat out again, but neither of them moved to make purchases.

"Why?"

Frankie wondered how best to explain it, wondered more why she felt so compelled to make him understand this wasn't merely a vindictive witch hunt. "The last time Mom and I talked about my dad was at his funeral. I admit there's no such thing as rational during a time like that. I needed to understand why she hadn't been more vocal about his innocence."

"Did it ever occur to you he might've been guilty?"

"Absolutely not." To believe that went against everything she knew about her dad's character and integrity. She didn't care if that skewed her perspective.

"Frankie." Aidan took her hand and guided her past buckets of bright, happy snapdragons that mocked the misery inside her. "We've picked up some company. We need to start shopping while we talk."

She blinked, momentarily startled by the instruction. A quick glance and she thought she'd pegged one. "The guy across the street with the paper?"

Aidan nodded. "And one on our six." He chose a dozen snapdragons and pulled out his wallet. "Is there a vase at the apartment?" His movements gave them time to assess the men tailing them.

"If not, we'll improvise." She pushed her mouth into a smile to match his and felt that feminine flutter grow. If her mother would just come clean, none of this would be necessary and Frankie wouldn't be stuck knowing the best romance of her life was a complete fraud.

He handed her the flowers so he could pull

out his phone. They looked at it together, just another couple consulting an electronic list as they checked the camera in the apartment. "Clear," he said, for her ears only. "Fieldwork can be such fun."

It made her laugh. "We can't let this take six months."

"You think it will be such a hardship to live with me?"

*Not at all.* The thought scared her. "I'd ask for hazard pay," she teased to lighten her mood. "I meant being this close to my mom. I'll crack if I have to play nice that long."

They strolled up and down aisles of vegetables, making choices and planning meals. Learning what tastes they had in common and where they differed. It was ridiculously real.

"Frankie, I'm begging you to be patient here," he said, standing too close while she selected fresh greens. "If you want the truth, you have to look at things objectively."

"You seem determined to repair a broken family. That isn't why we're here."

He was quiet as they started back up the hill to their building. The silence suited her, if only because he was right. She did have tunnel vision about Sophia. It would've been bad enough if her father had lived and been forced out of the army. She couldn't imagine the betrayal that drove him to suicide.

"When I asked her, point-blank, over my dad's grave, she said it was her fault."

Aidan stopped short and people flowed around them on the sidewalk. "That's a big detail to keep to yourself."

Frankie could just imagine what Victoria would think when he sent that in. "Would it change anything?" She shifted her hold on the grocery bags. "Sophia wouldn't explain and she refused to cooperate with anyone who could clear his name. I walked away and didn't speak to her again until yesterday."

"Give me those," Aidan said, taking the produce bags from her hands. "Did you consider that she was speaking figuratively?"

"That's the real question, isn't it?" Frankie picked up the pace, knowing he'd drop the subject when they reached the apartment. "I can't let her get away with it. When Dad's friend showed up, when he gave me the key, I made a choice to follow through, no matter what hell I discover on the way."

"I don't think it's that simple."

Frankie jerked open the building door with a harsh laugh. The strained sound bounced around the marble lobby. "Of course it isn't simple. Families and weddings never are," she added, just in case the security guard was on her mother's payroll. "But we'll get through it."

In the elevator, he set the groceries down and took her hands in his. The move rattled her until she remembered the security camera high in the corner. "Promise me you won't make a decision about any detail unless we talk about it first."

She opened her mouth to agree, but he silenced her with a soft kiss. The fleeting touch left her lips tingling.

"Don't just say the words, Frankie. Mean them."

"You can make the same promise to me, right?"

He nodded. "We're in this together," he said as the elevator doors parted at their floor.

*Together.* The team concept had always been important to her. An only child and an army brat, she put serious value in that word. For years, it had been the Leone family taking on the world. Then it had been the navy and her SEAL team. She'd recognized and battled loneliness through the years. She hadn't realized how deep it went until this moment. It was nice to know she wouldn't have to face the inevitable ugliness to come alone.

She wasn't sure if the revelation was a good thing or if she'd only be more broken when she and Aidan went their separate ways.

AIDAN STOOD BACK as Frankie unlocked their door. He didn't like being tailed any more than he liked the secrets Frankie was keeping. At least whoever was having them followed had yet to order a search of the apartment. He didn't count on the privacy lasting much longer.

There was a rhythm to this kind of work, and he could sense something was about to give. He'd handled delicate cases before, played cat and mouse with some of Europe's worst offenders. This was an entirely different scenario.

As they put away the groceries and tossed around dinner ideas, he hoped they sounded like a normal, contented couple. Her mother believed it, which mattered more than how being this close, this affectionate with Frankie was driving him mad. Although Frankie followed his lead when he made romantic gestures, he was going to have to encourage her to reach for him once in a while. He didn't dwell on the potential minefield of that thought.

He was relieved when she walked out to the balcony to take a call from Sophia. The line between his undercover role and his true feelings was blurring. He liked Frankie's spunk and admired her determination, even if he thought she was off target about her mom.

In Victoria's office, he'd seen a hurt, unhappy and angry woman. In Sophia's house, he'd watched the memories—good and bad—swamp her. Though he'd merely skimmed the surface of the classified morass that was the Leone family history, what he'd found confirmed that she'd been raised in a happy, stable home.

Frankie walked back in, tapping her phone against her palm. "Mom asked about setting a wedding date."

He smiled despite the chill slithering down his spine. "And?" Just because the gear hadn't picked up any active bugs didn't mean they could relax. If they were going to complete this investigation effectively, he might have to reserve a hotel room under an alternate name just so they could speak freely.

"And do you have a preference?" She slid onto the counter stool, watching him too closely.

Six weeks after never would be fine with him. "I thought girls spent most of their lives daydreaming about the perfect wedding."

"I'm a *woman*." Frankie crossed her arms and glared.

"I noticed." He came around the counter and grabbed her. "Anyone could be listening," he murmured at her ear, knowing that wasn't the point. Tipping up her chin, he planted a long kiss on her lips. For a moment she was shocked, her body stiff in his arms. Then she relaxed with a soft sigh that electrified his system. Her arms wound around his neck, and her fingers sifted through his hair. He forgot about the case as he slid his tongue between her lips and indulged in her warm, sensual taste. Need slammed through him, too tempting and far too convincing. He broke the kiss and smiled into her dazed eyes. "Name the date and time and you know I'll be there."

She slipped out of his reach, her face flushed and her lips plump from the kiss. "Mom suggested December. That gives us planning time."

He knew she was talking about the wedding as well as the case. How would a happy future groom reply? "You want to get married over the holidays?"

"There are lots of non-holiday days in December."

Was her irritation an act? Aidan glanced around the apartment. Although he was committed to the work, he didn't think anyone at the Colby Agency anticipated this assignment going for half a year. "Why not sooner?" he asked. The time crunch landed like a weight on his chest, making it impossible to get a breath.

"How soon can your family be here?"

*His family.* He knew she was teasing by the mischievous expression in her deep brown eyes. His eyes dropped to the ring on her hand. His gut clenched. Turning on his heel, he found a glass, filled it with cold water. Drink it or dump it on his head? He drank, buying time to think. Hashing over her past was part of the case. He wanted to keep his family, his mistakes to himself. Would Sophia respect his privacy or go snooping if he hedged on the family details? He knew the answer without asking.

He leaned back against the sink. "Does my family need to be here? I can call them after it's done. Send them a video of the ceremony. Live stream it."

"Aidan?"

The concern in Frankie's voice made him want to bolt. From the room and the case. Hell, from the planet. He struggled for control. "Tell her we'll look at the calendar," he said. "Tell her I'll reach out to my mom tonight." They both knew he wouldn't.

"Okay."

He had to trust the agency to field those calls properly, protecting their cover and shielding his parents from any unnecessary distress.

"We keep dancing around it, but if you think they won't like me, we can call this off. I don't want to come between you and your family."

"That's absurd." Hell, they'd probably love her under better circumstances. He stalked past her, wishing for something far stronger than the glass of water in his hand. He knew she was trying to stay in character. His problem was that she was suddenly so damned effective. Her eyes were his weakness. The woman needed his help whether she liked it or not, and he knew she didn't mean to hurt him.

"They'll adjust," he said. "They always do," he added under his breath, flopping down on the couch.

"To clarify, I'm not the one nagging." Frankie followed him, easing into the armchair. "If your parents aren't at your wedding, I think you'll regret it."

He could hardly tell her it wasn't any of her business, not here in a place likely wired for sound. "I'm familiar with the theory," he said. "We'll get it sorted out," he added, willing her to drop it.

"You haven't told them you proposed?"

Aidan stared at her, wondering if it was better to have this farcical conversation here, packed with double meanings she might not understand, or just take her out again and confess it all. They were likely under observation; they had to behave. He stayed on the couch, rolling the cool glass between his palms. "I haven't told them anything about you," he said quietly, testing her reaction. She would know that much was true. Whoever might be listening in would wonder why he'd lied to Sophia.

Frankie nodded. "All things considered, that's understandable."

A warning bell clanged through his head. "What?" He couldn't believe she'd diverted her relentless focus from her mother long enough to snoop through his past.

"As soon as you tell them you're seeing someone, that you're engaged, they'll pester you with questions. Being under my mom's microscope is enough pressure for us right now."

"I'm not going to crack."

"That's not what I'm saying." Frankie kicked off her shoes and tucked her bare feet up under her skirt. Reaching up, she pulled the clip holding her hair back and the silky dark waves tumbled over her shoulders.

He couldn't stop staring. The feminine, flowy dress and her loose hair softened the lean, tough woman. After his personal life had imploded, he'd never thought to be this emotionally intimate with anyone—personally or professionally. "Then be clear. I'm not in the mood for cryptic," he said, ignoring the irony.

She rolled her eyes. "I've seen it happen with friends. As soon as you let others into the relationship—just by saying you're involved with someone—it ups the expectations."

"You should expect more of me now that we're engaged." He tried to laugh it off.

"Stop growling like a bear." She came over, easing down beside him in that careful way she had. "I'm saying it's okay if you don't tell your parents anything until you're ready. We're not in any rush."

His pulse kicked as her ginger-and-clove scent washed over him. "But we'll keep lying to your mom when she's pressing for dates and plans?"

"I'll tell her to back off." Frankie picked up his hand and rested it on her knee as if they were really together. "You've gone the extra mile for me." She held up her left hand, flashing the ring and a wry smile. "It's my turn. Let's make a promise we won't let anyone else dictate what we want our life to look like."

Despite knowing the words were for a faceless listener, they soothed him. *She* soothed him. This was dangerous territory he'd entered and he couldn't see the exit. "I was engaged once before." It was too late to snatch the words back. Maybe if he opened up, she'd trust him a little more. "I never wanted to tell you."

Her dark eyebrows arched high, her eyes wide. "You don't have to tell me. It doesn't matter."

It mattered. Why hadn't he told her on the plane and avoided all this? He stroked his thumb along her ring finger, remembering another woman. "My family might not want to be around my wedding at all." She needed to hear the story just in case Leo Solutions got a peek behind the credentials the Colby Agency had created for him. "I met her through a friend," he began. "Call us foolish, but we went from introductions to engaged in about two seconds flat."

Frankie had the grace to blush.

"My family adored her. They were thrilled I was settling down, and thought being married would change my career goals."

"It didn't." She squeezed his hand, her eyes full of sympathy.

Between her upbringing and her career, she understood what he was saying despite what he left unsaid. It was a strange sensation. Though the case that killed his fiancée was officially closed and sealed, the guilt would follow him forever. "If we'd met while you were still in the navy, would we even be here now?"

"I doubt it," she said, her lips twitching into a wry grin. "My team never had much reason to be in Savannah."

At her joke, something like relief loosened the knot in his chest. Recognizing his honesty, she comprehended the concept of what had happened, as well as the lingering effects.

He might be able to play the part of a doting fiancé, but he'd never let another relationship get serious enough to put a woman at risk. "You've figured it out. She became a target." He kept his gaze on the window just past Frankie's shoulder. The memories assaulted him, anyway. "I couldn't save her. Our families were devastated by the loss. You know how it is. Hard words walk side by side with that kind of grief."

"Aidan. It's okay."

It wasn't. "Despite all that, I couldn't change who I am, what I'm good at."

"No one should ask you to change."

He couldn't stand the look on her face. Suddenly he wanted the sharp, tough Frankie, the woman impatiently searching for answers. He needed her to push him away. Instead, he pulled her body across his and kissed her, pouring all his frustration and desire into that sweet contact. Silently promising he wouldn't fail her as he'd failed others.

She didn't shove him away, but responded instantly, matching his urgency with her mouth and hands. He wrapped his arms tight around her, clinging until she was his only thought, his only awareness, his very breath. She knew his worst secret, his biggest failure, and she kissed him as if he was her hero.

Her head fell back and he feasted on the golden column of her throat. Her skin was so soft, with a trace of sweetness that was so at odds with her tough nature and determination.

"I love this dress," he said, slipping his hand under the hem to caress her knee, her firm thigh.

She trapped his hand with hers, stopping his progress. The move brought him back to his senses. He leaned away enough to enjoy the view of her stunning face. The personal and professional lines between them were more than blurred; they'd been obliterated. He forced himself to release her before he completely lost control. He'd never expected their performance, their *lies*, to get into his head this way. "I think I'll check out the gym." Awkwardly he pushed himself to his feet, left her there.

"I'll change and go with you."

He shook his head. "I'm okay. I'd like some space."

She sat up, smoothing her skirt, then her hair. "I'll work on dinner."

"Thanks." He shoved his hands into his pockets because he wanted to stay, to touch her and never quit. "I hope my past doesn't, um, change anything."

"Not a chance," she replied, busying herself with one of the throw pillows. "I'll come up with something so my mom doesn't pester you."

"You're a terrific fiancée." *In any context*, he thought. "I'll be back within the hour." He escaped to the bedroom and changed clothes, still reeling from that kiss. He left the apartment without risking another word. Taking her in his arms had nothing to do with possible spy devices and everything to do with the heat she stirred inside him. If he didn't stick with logic, if he didn't find his balance, the investigation could fall apart. Aidan had no idea what he'd do without the work and shelter of the Colby Agency.

What had possessed him to be so damned honest with her? If he'd told her that on the plane or in the jewelry store, she might have backed off the stupid engagement idea. Although, based on what he'd seen so far, she'd been right to take that angle. It gave her mother something happier to focus on than their difficult last meeting.

Aidan knew better than most how survival often hinged on finding a purpose beyond the tragedy. Her mother had done it, creating the business. Frankie had used the intention of clearing her dad's name to empower her full recovery. He knew how she felt. His dogged hunt for his fiancée's killer had been excused as a search for justice. Only the intervention of cooler heads had saved him from himself. He decided he was here not just as an investigator, but to be that same voice of reason for Frankie.

To follow Victoria's orders he had to stay close and protect Frankie from herself as much as her drive for answers. Surely he could find a way to do his job and keep his hands off her, at least when they were alone.

# Chapter Eight

*Monday, April 11, 7:15 a.m.*

Frankie had never wanted a hotel room more than she did on Monday morning. In the hotel they didn't have to talk in code or maintain the act 24/7. It irritated her that they couldn't be sure of anything right now. That kiss never would've happened at the hotel, where they could be themselves. It had taken all her self-control to pretend that delicious, groping contact on the couch hadn't fazed her.

Already Aidan knew better than to try to talk with her before her first cup of tea in the morning. She needed quiet time to wake up. Time to adjust her back and her attitude before attacking the day.

When she wandered into the kitchen, he slid a cup of tea in front of her. He was working on a plate of eggs with slices of crisp bacon on the side. "Help yourself."

She shook her head as she sipped the hot brew. She'd never been able to eat first thing in the morning. By the time he finished his breakfast her nerves were frayed. Neither of them said much until they got to the car. It already felt like a long day and they hadn't reached the office.

"Nervous?" she asked as he started the engine. Being the new kids at the company would be interesting. How would the employees react to the prodigal daughter and her future husband?

"Not at all."

"How can you say that?"

"Toughest part for me was our conversation yesterday."

Every ounce of courage she possessed had been required to keep her mind off that subject. She couldn't dwell on what he'd told her or how she'd lost herself in his embrace afterward. It was too much. "I'm sorry. If—"

"No apologies," he said, interrupting her. "Your tactic is working and we'll have more freedom at the office."

"We hope." She twisted the ring on her finger again. "Sophia's waiting for me to bring it up."

"I disagree. She's waiting to hear you'll stay and be part of her life and company."

Frankie ignored the little voice in her head that said he was right. "I didn't think the company would be this extensive. I know we studied it, but during the tour it felt so much bigger in person."

"Should make for an interesting morning," he said. "We've both faced tougher tasks."

"I know." Even before he'd shared his personal tragedy, she'd checked on the public records of his time with Interpol. Aidan had been involved in closing several important cases. As much as she'd resented it, Victoria had provided the perfect investigator for this case. Frankie suspected she always did. "Thanks again for being here."

"Says the woman who wanted me to stay away."

"Don't gloat," she said as he parked the car in the space Sophia had assigned them. "Without you, I would've lost my composure a dozen times by now."

"So few?"

"I understand the need for discretion and secrets. I don't understand why she persistently lies to me. If we prove that she helped convict an innocent man, what kind of person does that make me? I'm her daughter."

"Whatever your mom has or *hasn't* done, her actions don't change anything about you, Frankie."

She paused, her hand on the door handle, and allowed his words to sink in. It was basic logic and only more evidence that she was letting her emotions and family memories cloud her view of the present. "No offense, but I want to get in there and catch her red-handed so we can go back to our regularly scheduled lives as soon as possible."

His blue eyes narrowed. "That's a dangerous bias during an investigation."

Frankie shrugged. "You're the investigator. I'm just a daughter searching for the truth." With that she picked up her purse and left the car.

"Hang on." Aidan quickly caught up with her. "We agreed to do this the right way."

"And we will," she replied, her gaze straight ahead. "When we can prove she set up my dad, I will see it through every step of the legal process." Frankie was determined to find facts her mother couldn't explain away. Facts, and the resulting anger, were easier to deal with than the big question hovering in the shadows: Why? Her every memory featured her parents as happy and affectionate. Loving, devoted to each other in their careers and at home. Had her entire upbringing, her concept of love and relationships, been a web of deceit?

She pasted a smile on her face when she spotted her mother waiting for them at the information desk in the lobby. "Good morning!" Sophia embraced them both. "I thought I'd show you around before I turn you over to Human Resources."

Frankie started to remind her they'd had a tour on Saturday afternoon and had done the new-hire paperwork online, but Aidan spoke up first. "That's thoughtful, Sophia. Thanks."

It became immediately apparent her mother wanted to personally introduce them to everyone in the company, if not the building. Frankie knew she'd forget names, but not the floor plans or office locations.

They were with HR through the morning, and by lunchtime Frankie was hoping for a hearty meal and some quiet. Instead, Paul and Sophia picked them up and led them to the building cafeteria. Once again Aidan carried the conversation while Frankie concentrated on eating for the sole purpose of fueling up for the afternoon ahead.

"Frankie, your office is down the hall from mine," Sophia said as they wrapped up the meal.

"Office?" She hadn't expected that.

"I'll show you your space," Paul said to Aidan.

"It doesn't have much of a view, but you'll be near the training facilities."

"Makes perfect sense," Aidan said.

Frankie's stomach churned. She had the distinct impression that neither she nor Aidan would be allowed to roam Leo Solutions unsupervised. Had her mother seen through their act?

"Tonight we can have dinner and you can fill us in on your first day over grilled salmon."

"That'll be great, Mom," she said, stifling her reluctance. More socializing meant more of Aidan's tempting touches. "Can we bring anything?"

"Not at all." With a winning smile for Paul, Sophia stood up and motioned for Frankie to follow.

Aidan didn't let her go without a soft kiss on her cheek. "Have a great day," he said with a wink.

"I'm so glad you're here," Sophia told her as they rode the elevator upstairs. "Your father and I wanted this to be a family business."

Frankie swallowed back the grief and temper, remembering Aidan's words of caution. "Do you miss him?" It sounded like a daughter question to her.

Sophia's eyes turned sad and the wistful smile was either genuine or well rehearsed. "He was a good father, a good man, Frankie. I'm so sorry you didn't get the closure you needed."

The elevator doors parted and not even Frankie wanted to push the topic with so many curious eyes and ears aimed their way.

"Here's your office," Sophia said, stopping halfway down the long corridor. She opened the door wide and gestured for her to walk in. "Feel free to order the supplies you need. You'll remember my office is at the end of the hall."

Frankie just stared at the space. The surface of the desk gleamed and the only items on it were a computer monitor and a notepad. Of course her mother would remember how much she detested clutter. "Thanks," she murmured.

"I didn't order a nameplate yet. I wasn't sure if you were going to use your nickname here. I assume you'll take Aidan's last name when you marry."

"Right," Frankie said, walking around the desk toward the luxurious chair. "You really went all out."

"I want you to love it here," Sophia admitted, pushing the door closed behind her. "I know how disappointed you were by the navy's decision. You are your father's daughter."

"You can say that, when you believe he committed treason?"

"I've been waiting for that." Sophia sighed,

stepping a little closer. "Sweetheart, you have his drive and ambition. The charges and verdict are irrelevant. You need to let it go."

"How?" Frankie stopped herself just short of an angry rant, gripping the back of the chair. "He was disgraced, Mom. It haunts me."

"In the military it might have," she allowed. "It didn't haunt you in Savannah and it won't haunt you here."

"I'm not talking about career paths."

"I know." Sophia folded her arms and sighed. "If I had the answers, I'd share them."

Like the little girl she'd been, Frankie wanted to believe her. Wanted it so much she caught herself blinking away tears. She didn't trust her voice.

"Leo Solutions is built on a solid foundation," Sophia continued. "Yes, I had to shift the business plan after your father's problems, but we are stable. This company was his dream, our legacy to pass on to you." Everything about her relaxed as her lips curved in a tentative smile. "And here you are at last."

Here she was, all right, Frankie thought. Ready to excavate any and all secrets and dirty laundry propping up this company.

"Take a seat," Sophia urged her. "When you log on you'll have access to our previous proposals as well as what we've pulled together for the current one. If you have any suggestions, let me know. We'll be having meetings all week to get this one just right."

"Okay." She wished she could take the office, the job and the warm welcome at face value. It scared her how much she missed the mother she'd known and looked up to as a kid.

"I'm counting on your analysis and insight." Sophia tucked her hair behind an ear and set her earring swaying.

Frankie recognized the nervous move. "Anything else?"

"You have full access to every detail of the company. I'll be honest—Paul was against that decision. I insisted. This company will be yours one day."

*Hers?* If Aidan had found that in his research, he'd kept it to himself. "Thanks, Mom." The highs and lows of the day were getting to Frankie and she sank into the chair. "I appreciate your faith in me." The lies between them were knee-deep by now.

When Sophia left, Frankie wasted no time logging on and getting to work on both the tasks her mother expected her to address and her real purpose for being here. By midafternoon, she had full comprehension of the company's roots, as well as a general feel for their largest clients in both cyber and personal security. She downplayed the sense of accomplishment that reminded her of her navy days. This position naturally ran to her strengths of gathering intel and organizing it quickly.

The new contract Paul had the entire company focused on was more than lucrative; it would establish Leo Solutions on a global scale. But something about the potential client felt familiar. Frankie used the gift of full access and dug deeper into previous proposals. As she researched, she had an excuse ready should anyone ask why she was poking around the legal side of Leo Solutions.

At last she stumbled on something Aidan needed to see: a photo of her mom, Paul and the man who was now on the board of directors for the potential client Paul was determined to sign. The picture had been taken in Iraq. Frankie vaguely remembered her mother taking that trip as part of a delegation while American troops were shifting responsibilities to local authorities.

"Thank God for electronic storage," Frankie murmured. The picture had been included in a media piece covering the Leo Solutions opening and its positive impact in the Seattle area.

It would require more research, and Aidan's expertise and contacts overseas to confirm, but this client could become more of a threat than a boon. One of the company's subsidiaries had been in the news last year for making charitable donations that wound up funding terrorism in the Middle East. Follow-up articles claimed the problem had been rectified and reparations made. Frankie couldn't shake the bad feeling.

Why push it? The influx of cash would never offset the blow to Leo Solutions' credibility if anyone found out they provided cutting-edge cyber security for this group. Her mother couldn't have overlooked this blatant connection. What were she and Paul up to?

Frankie took pictures of the images and documents with her phone to share with Aidan later. After she also downloaded the files to her flash drive, she headed downstairs to find him.

His office door was open and for a moment she just enjoyed the view of him working. Not even the drab company uniform toned down the lure he presented. Her lips warmed at the memory of his mouth claiming hers. She knocked before she lost her nerve and retreated back upstairs. "Got a minute?"

When he turned toward her, the furrow of concentration between his dark eyebrows faded. "For you I've got all the time in the world."

She wanted to tell him to stop it but wisely

kept her mouth shut. "I might have a better view," she said, "but the furnishings are pretty much the same."

"Paul told me Sophia called in big favors with the office supply place to get us set up this morning."

"How are things down here?"

"You're just work, work, work. I don't know if I like it," he teased. "Come here and give me a kiss."

She rolled her eyes as she moved around to his side of the desk. "We should be setting a better example, Mr. Abbot."

"I'll wait to apologize until we get reprimanded, thank you." He caught her hand in his. "What did you need?"

It felt so close to normal she wanted to linger in the performance. "I found a recipe online." She pulled out her phone and showed him the pictures. "Maybe for tomorrow night, since we're going to Mom's tonight. What do you think?"

He scrolled through and when he looked up at her he was all smiles. "I think you could've emailed me."

"Well, I could have." Her tone was flirtatious. They both knew she couldn't risk leaving that kind of trail. His comment was for whoever was listening and potentially watching. She was getting used to their double-meaning conversations. "But then I would've missed your reaction."

"That has potential," he said. "Where'd you find it?"

"It was one of those email newsletters," she fibbed. "You could show a little more enthusiasm." Surely he understood the implication of what she'd found.

"I'll withhold judgment until I taste it."

He was reminding her not to jump to the obvious conclusion. Though this seemed crystal clear to her. "Fine."

He slid a hand over her thigh and she stopped the motion just before he reached one of the many scars. Recalling how she should react, she smiled and kissed his cheek. "We're at work," she said in a stage whisper as she escaped to the safe side of the desk.

"Can't wait until we're not." His eyes flashed with that attraction and awareness she couldn't deny. Her fingertips tingled as though she'd been playing with fire.

"I'll meet you at the car at five."

"I'd rather pick you up at your office and walk down together. I can carry your books if you have homework."

Shaking her head at his antics, Frankie returned to her office and the work her mother expected of her. She couldn't afford to alienate anyone or squander the access she hadn't anticipated.

ON THE DRIVE to the apartment, Aidan let her theorize about what she'd found, unable to find any flaw with her concerns. While she changed clothes, he took another look at the pictures and skimmed every article he could find, taking one last minute to email a friend of his at Interpol.

What Frankie wanted to see as proof positive, Aidan saw as coincidence, until they had independent confirmation the picture looked like proverbial smoke. He had yet to pin down anything that resembled a fire. Paul and Sophia could very well be trying to help a friend overcome and take positive strides forward. But his opinion was met with a stony silence.

He pulled into Sophia's driveway and parked behind Paul's sedan. Frankie stared straight ahead, her frustration clear in the tight fists balanced on her thighs. He'd expected her to use the time in the car to launch another debate about her discovery. "You'll be okay during dinner?"

"What's not okay?" She gave him a patently false smile. "We're all nearly family, right?"

He didn't like the hard edge she put on *family.* "We don't have to stay long."

"Of course we do," Frankie countered. "This is a great chance to dig into Paul's background."

That made Aidan wary. "Are you bucking for a confrontation?"

"No way. It's too soon. I just want to know how *they* wound up building my dad's dream."

"Your parents dreamed up Leo Solutions together."

Frankie closed her eyes a moment and let loose a weary sigh. When she opened them again her gaze was sharp enough to cut glass. "Be warned, she's going to push for a wedding date. I told her we weren't in a rush, but apparently she is."

"I'll manage." He took her hand. "Do we need a safe word?"

"What?"

"If one of us gets in trouble or wants to bail, maybe we should have a code word or phrase so it's not obvious."

Her gaze drifted to the house, and her dark eyebrows plummeted into a scowl. "Not a bad idea."

"Baby," he said.

"Do *not* call me that," she snapped.

"Which makes it a perfect code word," he clarified, holding up his hands in surrender.

"Oh. Okay." With a resigned expression, she climbed out of the car and headed for the porch.

Right on her heels, he caught the subtle way she adjusted her stride at the steps, as if she anticipated pain with the short climb. "Are you feeling all right?"

She glared at him over her shoulder but didn't answer as her mother opened the door wide to welcome them in. Paul was at her shoulder and hugs and handshakes were exchanged.

Aidan seconded Frankie's reservations about Paul. He picked up a bad vibe from the older man, as if he didn't want to share Sophia or the company with Frankie or anyone else.

"We've got the salmon going out back," Sophia said. "I have drinks and appetizers to tide us over."

Aidan noticed Frankie didn't even turn her head as they passed the formal dining room and the family portrait that had tripped her up during their first visit.

When the four of them were situated around a teak outdoor table sharing a plate of baked Brie and fruit, Aidan leaned back and draped his arm across the back of Frankie's chair. On the other side of the table, Paul mirrored the move with Sophia.

"What kind of flowers are those?" Aidan nodded at the flowering vines climbing the pergola.

"Moonflower," Frankie replied, sliding a

glance at her mom. "Do you have a spot for sunflowers here?"

"Yes!" Sophia pointed to the other side of the yard. "That corner gets plenty of sun. I'm thinking of adding a swing or bench nearby."

"She means I'll have a new building project soon," Paul added.

As Sophia launched an unconvincing protest, Aidan asked Frankie about the sunflowers.

"We found a place to plant them whenever we moved."

"It was part of making each house a home, wasn't it?" Sophia smiled.

Frankie nodded, clearly uncomfortable.

"You'll have so much fun creating your own traditions with Aidan," her mom noted.

"They don't have any green space in the apartment," Paul observed.

"Aidan and I were just talking about starting a container garden on the balcony," Frankie said.

He nodded, supporting her improvisation. "Maybe you could share some plants, if that's how it works."

"What a great idea," Sophia said, twisting in her seat as if assessing the best choices.

"Wouldn't it be better all the way around to find your own place?" Paul queried, raising his drink to his lips.

Aidan watched him as Sophia insisted "the kids" were welcome to stay in the apartment as long as necessary. "Are you still driving the rental car?" she asked.

"We've been debating what to do about that," Aidan improvised.

Sophia nudged Paul, who said, "We can set you up with a company car."

"Mom, that's too much." Frankie patted Aidan's knee. "There's plenty of time to figure it out."

Aidan caught the flash of satisfaction on Paul's face, then did the mental calculations of buying a car for the sole purpose of the case. It wasn't impossible if he was smart. Driving back to Chicago when the job was done wasn't the worst scenario. Just as Frankie wanted to avoid living with her mother, Aidan didn't want to be saddled with a company car.

He and Frankie had enough stress with the assumption that the apartment was wired. A company car would have active GPS at the very least, if not a dash cam or mic that would pick up every word they exchanged. They needed more space to speak privately, not more places where they had to play the happily engaged, electrically attracted couple.

Sophia enlisted Paul's help getting the salmon to the table, and the delicious meal kept everyone distracted for a time. Frankie surprised Aidan by conversing amicably with Paul and her mother, getting both to open up—in the vaguest sense—about their friendship and the partnership.

Aidan hadn't expected her to have such a deft touch with those questions. Sophia so obviously wanted Frankie and her fiancé to feel welcome. She wanted them to stay and was doing everything possible to nurture the olive branch Frankie had offered by showing up.

It would make Sophia miserable if she guessed her daughter's real purpose here. He had a feeling it would make Frankie miserable, too, if she found something to confirm her worst suspicions about her mother. She might believe she wanted to take her mom down, but Aidan wasn't convinced.

"So, have you decided on a wedding date?"

Frankie, caught off guard, lowered her loaded fork back to her plate. Under the table, he rubbed her knee with his for encouragement. "Not specifically," he answered. "Are there dates we should avoid?"

Sophia's dark hair swung gently as she shook her head. "I don't think so. Paul?"

He shrugged and dropped his gaze to his plate. "Whatever suits the happy couple."

"Do you have your heart set on a particular venue, Frankie?"

Beside him, Aidan felt Frankie tense up. "I really haven't thought about it. Being engaged is enough for us right now," she added, sticking with the excuse she fell back on whenever the topic came up.

He recalled her comments about expectations and realized what she meant. No one in either family had been quite this pushy after he proposed before. There hadn't been time. Shortly after the engagement parties they were planning a funeral rather than a wedding.

"We need to get started," Sophia said. "The best places are likely booked for June."

Frankie coughed and reached for her water glass.

While she sputtered, Aidan jumped into the fray. "June feels terribly quick. I'd marry her anywhere, anytime," he added, when Sophia's happy expression faltered. "To do it right, maybe we should look to the fall?"

"That would give your family more time to make travel arrangements," Sophia said. She glanced at Paul. "Maybe we can help with some of that. The company has an account with a charter airline service."

"Really?" Frankie asked. "I didn't realize we had clients that required so much travel."

Paul blotted his mouth with his napkin and set it beside his plate. "Primarily the charter service empowers accounts where personal security arrangements are necessary. Your mother and I worked out a strategy to give the company a global reach and relevance right away."

Sophia nodded, immediately returning to her preferred topic. "If your family comes all this way, I hope they'll take some extra time for enjoying the city in addition to the wedding."

"I'll certainly suggest it," Aidan said, once more grasping Frankie's hand. Despite his plan to take a step back, he couldn't quite keep his hands to himself. Of course, in public it was considered part of the job, he thought, justifying the pleasure he felt in the contact.

"Are there dates that are important to your family, Aidan?" Paul asked.

Aidan recognized the veiled interrogation. "My parents were married in late September."

"A lovely time of year." Sophia's smile bloomed on her face, and her eyes crinkled with happiness. "Would you like a September wedding, Frankie?"

"That could work." She squeezed Aidan's hand. "Just don't get your hopes up for anything big like the officers' club," she said. "We'd prefer something simple."

Aidan watched the barb land perfectly. Sophia's enthusiasm dipped momentarily. "We can manage a simple, tasteful day that suits you both."

"We could just go to the courthouse," Frankie suggested, looking up at him. "What do you think?"

He wasn't about to let her off the hook or give her mom heart failure. "We could manage that next week," he pointed out, calling her bluff.

Frankie blanched. "Or in September, after we settle in here."

"Absolutely not," Sophia protested. "I only have one daughter, and while it's your day, I want it to be a celebration you'll remember."

Aidan decided this was another woman, family and case he'd never forget.

Sophia wagged a finger at her daughter. "Pull up a calendar and choose a date. It will give us a target even if we have to adjust it." The woman sounded as though she'd been the general in the family.

Obediently Frankie did as requested, and she and Aidan chose the last Saturday in September to appease the mother of the bride.

Aidan expected to feel snared. Instead, he heard himself laughing as he leaned over and kissed Frankie's temple. "Always a good idea to have a target for any successful operation. Does it feel too real, my love?"

"Maybe a little." She elbowed him in the side and had all four of them grinning. "Just wait. You won't be laughing when we're confronted with dozens of choices over the smallest details."

"You know I trust your judgment." As he said the words he realized how true they were. Not just as her pretend fiancé. Watching how she'd handled this evening, he knew she'd play this investigation the smart way: patiently, until they had the necessary evidence to take action against the right person.

While Frankie would surely disagree, he was increasingly confident Sophia wasn't that person.

"I NEED A RUN," Frankie said as they entered the apartment. She wanted some space to sort out the crazy day and crazier dinner. In the navy, she'd never been required to maintain this sort of cover. The assignments had been handed out, planned and executed. There were gaps and improvisations, of course, but she'd never had to second-guess every breath the way she did now.

"You're going to the gym downstairs, right?"

"No." She stalked past Aidan, grabbed her running gear and ducked into the bathroom to change. He was sitting on the bed, glaring at her when she emerged. "What now?"

"You can go to the gym," he declared.

She laughed. "I'm a big girl, Aidan. I'm going running outside."

"Not alone at night."

"You're overprotective all of a sudden," she said, for the benefit of any prying surveillance. Reaching into her drawer, she showed him her knife, then tucked it into the sheath clipped at her waist. She tugged her T-shirt down to hide it. "I won't be long."

"We'll go together." He stood and she back-pedaled out of the room before he could catch her or kiss her into submission.

"No." She gathered her hair into a ponytail. Frankie could hardly confess she needed to escape him. It seemed his intriguing scent filled her every breath. Here, in the car, at dinner. She had to stretch her legs, let her mind wander and just be herself for a bit. "I'll be back within the hour."

"Frankie—"

"I'm going alone. You won't change my mind."

"Fine." He scowled at her. "At least take your cell phone."

With a sigh, she grabbed it and dashed out the door. Considering it a good warm-up, she took the stairs down for a few flights, pausing to stretch on the landings.

Outside, the cool night air washed over her

and she drew in a deep breath as she set out down the block toward a nearby green space that flowed along the waterfront. Using the app on her phone, she programmed a route that circled back to the building. That way she wouldn't be tempted to stay out later just to annoy Aidan.

Probably not smart to alienate her only ally in town. If she could call him that. He kept insinuating she wasn't capable of objectivity. It stung, knowing he was right. But couldn't he put himself in her shoes for just a few minutes?

The man had been a top investigator in Europe and he was a whiz with undercover work. He should be able to see her point of view on this. How was she supposed to frame her life if everything she'd learned about love and strength, and all she'd known about the two people who'd mattered most, was false? In her place, up against these terrible questions, she couldn't imagine Aidan doing anything different.

She ran, letting the questions float through her mind, releasing the pent-up stress with every exhale. Her father had been relocated to Washington during her senior year of high school. She and her mother had stayed behind so she could finish school with her friends. Had that decision also been motivated by trouble in their marriage Frankie hadn't seen?

She concentrated on her footfalls, rather than get sucked into that quagmire. She was out here to escape the situation, not wallow in it. Her legs were warm, her stride strong and powerful, though she was mindful of the smallest twinge in her back.

She knew the difference between healthy and a signal to ease up and evaluate. Every step was a victory over the initial, bleak prognosis. Good thing she didn't believe in quitting. Her mother must have been told the odds were slim that Frankie would even walk again. Odds were no match for grit and determination, though the navy wouldn't believe her. Their loss, she thought as she pressed on, feeling the welcome strain in her lungs now.

She checked the route on her phone, thinking about Aidan's comments that Sophia had chosen to be with her in those early days. It was a point in her mom's favor that she'd never once told Frankie a full recovery was impossible.

Giving a nod to passing runners, she was tempted to snap a picture for Aidan. There was nothing to fear out here, especially not for an armed woman trained by the military's best experts. She didn't take the picture, nearly turned off her phone, except he'd likely call out a search party if she did that. The mental image made her smile. No one had cared so much about her survival since she left the navy. Aidan would probably tell her Sophia cared, but Frankie didn't want to think about her mother any more tonight.

At the two-mile mark, she hit the sweet spot where it felt as though she could run forever, and she let herself relax into her stride. Following the programmed route, she turned at the next path and looped around, dutifully heading back toward the apartment.

She sensed trouble just before it lunged out of the deep shadows between the trees. A man in a blue sweatshirt and gray athletic shorts, wearing a dark cap and bright white shoes, blocked her path.

"Gimme your money!" His demand was slurred around the edges, but she didn't smell any alcohol on him.

"Why?" She hoped the question would buy her precious seconds as she stutter-stepped closer to the next streetlamp. He kept his head low and moved to tackle her. She spun, letting him flow by her, drawing her knife. "Better luck next time," she said, racing down the path toward safety.

He chased after her rather than giving up. She kicked into high gear, but he matched her pace, finally bumping her off the paved trail and down a grassy slope.

Her phone fell, but her grip on the knife was sure as she rolled, coming to her feet braced for battle. He charged, gravity and momentum aiding his attack.

She drove an elbow into his ribs when he went high, but before she could follow through with a kick, someone else dragged her to the ground from behind. Her battle-starved heart swelled at the challenge of two opponents.

"Stay put," Aidan ordered, leaping between her and her assailant.

Not an opponent, a teammate. She jumped up, refusing to cower while he handled it. Confronted with losing odds, the mugger grabbed her phone and ran off.

Frankie started after him, but Aidan caught her around the waist. "Are you nuts? Let him go."

"He's got my phone!"

"It's replaceable. You aren't." Aidan's hands swept over her, checking her for injuries.

"Give it a rest. I'm fine." She was in no mood for an "in character" exchange. "There's evidence on my phone," she added in a furious whisper.

"I don't care."

She tucked the knife back into the sheath and started up the slope to the path. He fell into step beside her. "What were you thinking? I could've stabbed you."

He snorted. "You're welcome. I told you it wasn't safe out here."

She let her breath out in a slow hiss. It didn't calm her down. "If you'd been paying attention, you would've noticed I had it under control."

"Oh, right."

"I can't believe you followed me." She pulled the tie out of her hair and shook it loose as they walked along the path. Her scalp was sweaty and the confrontation pissed her off. Aidan's interference only exacerbated the anger beating through her veins.

"Good thing I did. He had fifty pounds on you."

"I had it under control," she repeated, flexing her hands. "Why couldn't you let me have this one hour to myself?"

"Because your safety is my priority."

"Bull. Victoria sent you along so I don't create more scandal than my father did."

"That's not true," he snapped.

"You promised me honesty." She broke into a jog, needing to get away from him. She couldn't look at him right now, didn't want to hear his voice. If she had any choice at all, she'd pack up and run to her mother's, claiming a lovers' spat. She was deep into that stupid scenario when

Aidan caught up with her again. He earned points for not speaking until they were a block from the apartment. "The bugs are live," he murmured. "And we've earned an upgraded team." His gaze slid past a dark van at the end of the block.

"I noticed the van when I set out."

"Did you use an app for your run?"

"Yes." Her temper dissolved as she realized what he was saying. "Good grief." She stopped short and he moved in as if they were swept away by a romantic moment. His lips on her cheek, brushing over her ear, almost derailed her train of thought. "You think someone purposely set that mugger on me to get my phone?"

Leaning back, Aidan smiled down at her, and her foolish heart tripped and fell over the concern and affection shining in his blue eyes.

"I do," he said. His palm was warm at the small of her back as he turned her toward the entry. "I like the sound of those two words together," he added as they crossed the lobby to the elevators. "Are you sure we can't just go to the courthouse this weekend?"

So he'd decided the building staff couldn't be trusted, either. At the moment, she shared his paranoia. "You heard Mom at dinner. She'd be heartbroken if we did that."

"Well, I don't want to be responsible for that."

"You've been such a good sport about all this," Frankie said, leaning into his touch as the elevator arrived. She might've gripped him a little tighter than necessary, but he didn't seem to mind. As they boarded the elevator, she murmured, "I'm still mad at you."

"Get over it quickly," he suggested. "Once we cross that threshold, we're 'on' again."

Knowing he was right didn't make it any easier.

"You should call the police," he said as they walked in, rolling his hand so she'd follow his lead.

"And say what? The guy didn't hurt me and we left the scene. I'll just buy a new phone."

"You could give them a description."

Frankie stared at Aidan, shaking her head and holding up her hands. What did he want her to say? "I guess you're right. I'll call after I get a shower."

She walked toward the bathroom and started the water. "This is silly," she murmured, when he followed her in so they could talk for a minute.

"If you've got a better idea, I'm listening," he said.

"Fine. We'll come up with a new option tomorrow." She leaned back against the counter and crossed her arms. "Still think that 'recipe' I found is useless?"

"I never thought it was useless." He leaned forward, his arms caging her between his broad, lean chest and the countertop. "Tell me you backed it up somewhere besides your phone."

If he was trying to intimidate her, it wasn't working. It was turning her on. She reached under her shirt, nearly laughing when he jerked back.

"What are you doing?"

"I'm not jumping you," she said with more than a little regret. She pulled a small flash drive out of her bra. "Giving you something to work with."

Turning one of his hands palm-up, she placed the drive in his palm and curled his fingers around it. "Now get out of here." She set her knife on the counter and plucked at her T-shirt. She refused to undress in front of him. Kisses were one thing, but she didn't want to see his face shift to disgust when he saw the scars and divots where chunks of muscles had been blown away. "I really want a shower." It was no business of his if it was cold.

"Right." His gaze trailed from her head to her toes and back up again. "Right."

"Aidan." She waved a hand in front of his face. "Go away."

He shook his head briskly. "I need one more thing."

"Wh—"

He interrupted her with a kiss, drawing her flush against his body as he laid claim to her mouth. She clutched his shoulders as much for balance as for the sheer pleasure. No one could hear them. No one was watching. This kiss was just for him. Or her. *Them.* She stopped trying to analyze the purpose and just enjoyed the sensual beauty of the moment. The night air lingered in his hair and she tasted the rich flavor of the beer he'd had at dinner. His lips, warm and tender, moved over hers, coaxed a delicious, instinctive response from her.

"When he jumped at you…" His voice trailed off and he dropped his forehead to hers. "I'm glad you had it under control."

"Kissing me doesn't make me less mad at you."

"I know." He grinned and her heart fluttered in her chest. "That's part of the attraction."

She gulped in a deep breath when he walked out. Held it. Released it slowly. She peeled away her sweaty clothes and stepped into the shower. The cold water poured over her, bringing her back to her senses. So much for keeping him at arm's length. If Aidan's career as an investigator stalled out, he had a promising career in acting.

Pressing her fingertips to her lips, she wondered which one of them he was trying to convince or distract, with expert kisses like that one.

# Chapter Nine

*Tuesday, April 12, 8:30 a.m.*

Aidan focused on the new job as soon as he hit the office Tuesday morning, catching up on the progress of trainees. He was searching the calendar for ways to implement his own ideas when Sophia's elegant shadow crossed his doorway.

"Good morning, Aidan."

He smiled at the woman who thought he'd be a son-in-law soon. "Good morning."

"I heard there was some trouble at the apartment last night. Is everything okay?"

He shouldn't be surprised she'd heard about the police report. Frankie and Victoria had warned him of Sophia's extensive connections, and he knew from experience that old habits were the last to die. "No trouble. Frankie performed a bit of community service during a run in the park."

"Pardon me?"

Aidan hesitated. "What exactly did Frankie tell you?"

"I haven't asked her. A friend of mine in the police department saw her name on an incident report. According to it, she fought off a mugger and lost her phone. I assumed, incorrectly apparently, that you'd give me the full story."

Aidan leaned back in his chair. She was being candid, so he'd follow suit. "I'm not comfortable getting between you and Frankie. On anything."

"Was she really out for a run?"

"Yes."

Sophia beamed. "I thought maybe she'd exaggerated when she said that the other day. The girl *never* gives up. They called it a miracle she lived through that first night." She fanned her face, tears brimming on her lashes. "Forgive me. I'm so glad to have my daughter back, so glad she's found happiness with you. You have no idea what it means to me," she said before she hurried away.

Aidan disagreed. He had a clear sense how much the daughter mattered to the mother. And he was increasingly convinced, Frankie's opinion of the evidence aside, that Sophia was the one in the dark. If she knew the apartment was bugged, if she knew they were being tailed, she was a pro at hiding it.

He heard Frankie's voice in his head, reminding him of Sophia's career as a military analyst, of her contribution to the alphabet soup district in Washington, DC. So far, she'd proved herself a loving mother above all else.

He didn't care about Sophia's past; he felt like an ass for deceiving the woman this way. Making it worse was the knowledge that his fake affection for Frankie was growing into a serious fascination compounded by intense desire. Every tiny detail she revealed left him wanting to discover more.

When the mugger had jumped her last night, Aidan had felt murderous. He'd woken with a start in the middle of the night and left the couch to check on her. As he watched her sleep, it had hit him that this was more complicated than keeping her safe to avoid a repeat of his past.

He was doing the one thing he'd sworn never to do again: he was falling in love.

UPSTAIRS, FRANKIE KEPT her attention strictly on the job today. Aidan had asked her to give him time to verify some details and make some calls. She was basically cooperating, even as she explored the documentation about the formation of the company. She had valid reasons if anyone questioned her, although her reasoning got a little weak when it came to how the documentation landed in her personal cloud storage.

Her email chimed with an instant message from her mother, asking for a private meeting in fifteen minutes.

Nervous that she'd been caught, Frankie forced herself to sit back and take a deep breath, then one more for good measure. She'd been granted full access. She hadn't done anything wrong. Her new job was to look at the past and present to help with a proposal for a future client. Satisfied with her logic, she checked her appearance and reached for her phone—which wasn't there, because she hadn't replaced it yet.

When Frankie walked to the end of the corridor, Sophia's assistant wasn't at her desk and the office door was open, so Frankie peeked in. But her mother wasn't there. Being perpetually early was a curse of being raised by a top general. Her stiff back was a by-product of her ambitious career and a restless night after the mugging, so Frankie decided to walk a lap around the floor rather than sit and let her muscles lock up.

She heard voices as she approached the stairs near the break room at the corner opposite Sophia's office.

"People get mugged in Seattle all the time."

Frankie recognized Paul's voice and froze, just out of sight.

"She's my daughter, not a random stranger."

"That doesn't warrant a protective detail. How many times have you told me she can take care of herself?"

"And she did," Sophia admitted. "I'm not pulling them."

"Sophia. Call them off," Paul insisted. "The rumors…"

"Don't exist," Sophia snapped. "Anyone working for *me* knows better than to talk about it."

*Talk about what?* Did that mean people working for Paul were chatty? The facts lined up in a shocking revelation. Her mom was responsible for the team tailing them? Frankie's stomach twisted and questions tumbled through her mind. It was all she could do to stand there when her body vibrated with the urge to confront them both.

"We can't afford to show any weakness," Paul said. "If this gets out, it could wreck everything."

"Please. Our clients have more sense than that."

"Sophia, think about it."

"I don't need to. I'm not pulling them until I'm sure."

Frankie gave herself a mental kick. If she'd had her phone, she could be recording this.

Aidan would have to reconsider Sophia's innocence when he heard about this exchange. Hearing them part ways, Frankie pushed open the stairwell door as though she'd just walked through it, turning for her mom's office.

Her palms were damp and her legs trembled, making her gait awkward. *Breathe, think, breathe.* She had to get herself under control before her mother spotted her.

"Oh, there you are." Sophia glided up, offering a half hug so Frankie had plenty of room to evade the contact. "How are you feeling today?"

She gave in and accepted the gesture. "Better than ever," she replied, pretending her mom wasn't privy to last night's problems.

"Aidan told me what happened," Sophia said, when they were alone in her office.

Frankie couldn't hide her surprise. "You spoke with him about me?" Why bother, when she'd hired a team to follow them?

"It wasn't like that," Sophia said quickly. "A friend of mine on the police force mentioned the report you filed. I know how you typically understate matters, so I asked Aidan about it."

Frankie folded her arms over her chest. "And you're asking me now in order to confirm his story?"

"No. He refused to tell me anything beyond the facts in the report. I can see you're okay."

Frankie immediately relaxed. She'd thank Aidan at the earliest opportunity.

"You've chosen a smart man," Sophia continued, muggers apparently forgotten as she crossed her office. A mobile wardrobe had been parked next to the couch by the window. She turned, fanning her face. "The way he *looks* at you, sweetheart. Well, it's reminiscent of my early days with your father. You're a lucky woman."

*"Mom."* Frankie's heart did a happy dance and she quickly reminded herself Aidan was an excellent actor. While it would've been a compliment years ago, now the comparison felt all wrong. Dirty. Could she use the opening and ask about what had changed between her parents to have her mother assist with the general's conviction? Frankie wanted the relationship answers nearly as much as the professional ones.

And Aidan had asked for time. She pushed her questions to the back of her mind. "What did you want to discuss?" she asked, pasting a smile on her face.

Sophia grinned. "Feel free to tell me if I've overstepped, but I called in a favor or two."

*To keep an eye on me*, Frankie thought. Eventually all this would come out. "Do I want to know?"

Sophia pulled back the curtain on the wardrobe. "I couldn't resist."

Wedding dresses. Frankie was stunned. There had to be twenty gowns, individually bagged and crammed tightly together on the rack. It was so unexpected she just stood there gawking.

"I know you think we have months," Sophia said, "but September will be here before you know it."

"We— I— Mom." She rubbed a fist along the ache at the front of her hip. "Mom, this is your office."

"I know it's silly, but I thought we could at least narrow down the styles you prefer." She held up a stack of magazines. "I bought out the bridal section on my way into work. And a few planning guides." She tapped a pile of thick books on the corner of her desk.

"You have wedding fever."

Sophia's enthusiasm drained away. "You're unhappy."

On too many levels to count, Frankie thought, feeling terrible. *Play the part.* It wasn't just her life or reputation on the line. If she faltered, Aidan would be screwed, too. That fear helped her sell it. "It's just so much." She gave the dresses her full attention. "Too much. We could've made an appointment."

"Please. I know you. You inherited a double

dose of drive and commitment from your father and me. The client proposal will be fine." She waved off the contract of the year as though it were an annoying fly. "Let's take half an hour for this."

"I can just imagine the staff's opinion of our meeting."

"I'd do this for any one of them," Sophia replied.

Frankie raised an eyebrow.

"Well," she amended, "maybe not this, precisely, but I take the time to know what's going on with my people. Now, tell me what you had in mind."

Frankie wondered how many surveillance teams Sophia had at her disposal. "I haven't had dresses in mind at all," she said. There wasn't room for much beyond her determination to clear her father. "No ruffles," she added, when her mother gave her an anxious look. "Simple is better."

"Clean lines. Got it." Sophia nodded and turned to the rack. "What about lace?"

Frankie struggled to come up with any fashion terms applicable to wedding gowns. "Wasn't your dress lace?"

"Yes," she said quietly. "It was fashionable at the time." She unzipped one of the garment bags. "Let's start with this one." She handed the gown to Frankie. The curtains that blocked the window to the rest of the floor were already closed. She locked the door and motioned for Frankie to undress.

"Here?"

"Our next appointment can be at the boutique with champagne and the works." Sophia waved her hands. "Come on, sweetie."

Frankie thought about the burn scars on her thighs and the surgical scars on her back and sides. She hadn't let anyone see them since the rehab hospital declared the wounds healed. "Can we just look at the dresses today? I'm not comfortable doing this in here. At the office," she added, hoping to appeal to her mother's work ethic.

Sophia studied her with one of those X-ray gazes only mothers possessed. "What is it? Talk to me, sweetie."

How could Sophia have her followed—possibly mugged—one minute and turn the office into a bridal boutique the next?

"It's not how I imagined it, that's all. I haven't imagined it," she said, hoping the right words would tumble out of her mouth if she kept talking. "You know I was never the little girl who dreamed of walking down the aisle."

"Is it the scarring?"

Frankie shivered at Sophia's astute guess.

"No," she lied. That was only vanity, anyway, though she'd forever think twice about wearing shorts and short skirts. "When my friend Jack got married, his wife had one of those big princess gowns with the, um, little tucks in the skirt." Jack had died in the attack that left Frankie wounded and paralyzed, but his wedding was the only one she'd attended. Hopefully his widow would forgive her for surviving.

"Here." Sophia put a bridal magazine in her hands and nudged her toward a chair. "Flip through that and dog-ear the pages that appeal to you. Don't analyze, just gut reactions."

Frankie obeyed, ignoring the slide of zippers and whooshes of fabrics behind her. Where was Aidan when she was in real trouble? Muggers were no problem compared to a determined mother of the bride.

"All right, turn around."

Again Frankie cooperated, helpless to remain aloof as Sophia beamed in front of a wall of white. "Do any of these resemble what you marked?"

There were gowns of every style, from a bell-skirted ball gown to a sleek and modern sheath with a band of sparkles at the waist. "Is it even possible to walk in a mermaid gown?" Frankie asked.

"I'll teach you, if it's the one," she promised. "All the more reason to choose early."

Unconvinced, Frankie walked over, standing by her mother to assess the dresses in the lineup. "I guess I like the sweetheart neckline," she said, flipping to a page in the magazine showing a similar style.

"Very romantic," Sophia said approvingly as she reached up and moved that dress to the far left. "Anything else?"

"I do want to try on an extravagant ball gown," Frankie admitted. "Just for fun. Aidan would laugh if I wore it," she lied. He wouldn't laugh, because they weren't getting married.

"Not a chance," Sophia declared. "I've never seen a man so adoring."

Frankie let that go, choosing two more gowns and handing her mother the magazine. Then she noticed the last dress. "Mom," she whispered. "That's *your* wedding dress."

Sophia smiled. "Your father swayed on his feet when he saw me. He never admitted it, but I was sure there were tears of joy in his eyes when I walked down that aisle. There's no pressure at all, but it might be a nice way to include him on your special day. We were married in May," she said, her voice full of memories. "It might not be right for a September wedding."

Overcome, Frankie barely kept it together as

she promised to try on the column of lace with a chapel train. She endured the calendar search for the right date for the boutique and then escaped to the safety of her office.

She leaned back against the closed door, her heart lodged in her throat and her hands quaking. Ages ago, when they were stationed in Europe, she'd gone ice-skating on a frozen river, her mitten-covered hand safe in her father's big palm. She remembered that day so clearly, the bite of the wind, the squeal of laughter when he spun her around. She remembered standing hand in hand with him weeks later, watching from the bank as the thinning ice cracked and split, to float away with the current.

She felt that way now. Cold. Fractured. Drifting on a course she couldn't control. She wanted to know which woman was the real Sophia Leone. Was it the savvy businesswoman who hired covert teams and kept state secrets, or the warm mother devoted to her family? Were Sophia's two sides mutually exclusive? Frankie caught her reflection in the window glass, hating the haunting similarities between mother and daughter.

She'd told Victoria the truth mattered above all. Ideally, she wanted to clear her father's name. Barring that, she wanted her mother's full explanation for the part she'd played in his downfall. Suddenly, Frankie wasn't sure what truth she wanted or even how far she was willing to go to hear it.

She should just march down the hall and confront her mom, demanding an answer for each of her suspicions. But giving in would be selfish and blow any chance of justice. A confession without evidence was useless. Worse, if she was wrong, she'd destroy her relationship with her mother—something she'd been so sure she could live without. Now the possibility of that finality frightened her.

Frankie turned away from the window and dropped to the floor behind her desk, where no one could see her. On her back, she pulled her knees to her chest and just rested there, searching for a solution.

When had doing the right thing become so twisted and complex? If her mother went to prison for her crimes, Frankie would be alone. If she told her mom everything and was wrong, she'd face the same solitary fate, with an extra helping of guilt for doubting her mother's motives and actions.

The statement from the safe-deposit box was clear. That picture from Iraq didn't lie. The conversation Frankie had overheard an hour ago confirmed something wasn't right.

She heard Aidan's voice in her head, urging

caution. The only time she'd mastered patience was during her navy career. Aidan had been involved in all this for a few days, while Frankie had been dealing with the storm cloud looming over her life for far too long. So why was she thinking about walking away? Could she spend the rest of her life pretending she'd come to terms with how her father died?

Which took precedence, family or country? She'd been raised by two people who preached the philosophy of God, country and family, in that order. Had her upbringing been a lie, and if so, what did that make her?

She closed her eyes, but her mother's face filled her mind. All her life Frankie had heard people say she had her mom's beauty and her dad's grit. She'd chosen the navy in an effort to make her own way, outside the reach of her father's influence and her mother's shadow.

What did it mean that so much of her identity and perception of self was tied up with two people who as of a year ago felt more like strangers?

Her office door opened with a soft squeak of hinges and Frankie opened her eyes. She might be new, but no one should feel free to walk in here without knocking. That someone had come snooping might turn into the break she needed.

She sat up and startled Aidan. "What are you doing?" Her question overlapped into his inquiry about whether she was all right or not. "Stop asking. I will let you know when I'm not feeling well."

"You're on the floor," he pointed out.

She clambered to her feet, hating the way her hip seized in the process. "I was thinking." He raised his eyebrows, but she refused to elaborate. "What brings you by?"

"Your mom suggested I take you to lunch."

"Why?"

"Beats me." He shrugged. "I'm just following orders."

"She's deliberately keeping me away from work today." Frankie made a fist and rubbed at the sore spot in her back. Rolling down the slope with the mugger had tweaked something. Not enough to matter, just enough to annoy.

Aidan looked to the ceiling. "She's watching out for you. She saw the police report."

"I heard."

"I'm glad she told you."

Frankie nodded. "Thanks for sticking up for me."

"Any fiancé worth his salt would do the same."

She was suddenly exhausted. "Is it bad form to go home early my second day on the job?"

"You're the boss's daughter." He tucked his hands into his pockets. "Let's have lunch and then you can ask me again."

During lunch, she told him about the conversation she'd overheard between Sophia and Paul. She kept the impromptu wedding dress exhibit to herself.

"I'll see what I can find on the team tailing us," he said. "Knowing Sophia planted them startles me."

Frankie let him have his objective delusions.

"Apartment or office?" he asked, when they finished eating.

"Office. I'll be damned if she keeps me out of there all day long."

"Frankie."

"I promise to behave, but I will get what I came for." It helped knowing he'd be researching, as well.

Back in her office, she sat down behind her desk and debated her options. There had to be something definitive. Something she and Aidan could agree on about her mother's involvement with her father's ruin.

What Frankie had considered black-and-white, starting with that damaging statement from the safe-deposit box, was becoming a foggy bank of gray. She was tired of words that weren't answers, weary of incomplete theories rolling around in her head. Frankie's focus narrowed to finding one inarguable piece of intel she could use to force her mother to talk.

She pulled up the research on crime trends and client services Leo Solutions had provided since opening its doors. Then she pulled up the current proposal. Present or past? Which research would pay off sooner?

Mentally, she flipped a coin, and wound up combing through her mother's email, for lack of any other option. Her mom was too smart to leave anything that might implicate her on the company server, but Frankie just wanted to see what was there.

The email address from a doctor caught her attention and Frankie dug a little deeper. The message, forwarded from Sophia's personal account, confirmed an appointment this afternoon. Frankie worked her way back through the correspondence, easily tracking the old trail of emails. Researching the doctor, she discovered he was a psychologist and her mother the patient.

Frankie wanted to give a victory shout. Something like this, in the wrong hands, could push Sophia out of the company and into an early retirement. As Paul had said earlier, investors and clients didn't like any sign of weakness at the top.

"Prepare for a shock, Mom," Frankie whispered. It would be a matter of a few keystrokes and Leo Solutions would be in serious trouble. "The truth will come out."

Better if she could figure out the connection and compel her mother to be honest—for once since her dad had died. Noting appointment dates, she was surprised they went back so many years. This wasn't a short-term grief counselor her mother had consulted to overcome anxiety during the recent family struggles. This was a long-term doctor-patient relationship that went back to when they'd moved to Seattle.

Troubled, Frankie switched gears, learning as much as she could from the doctor's website, skimming through articles ranging from marital counseling to drug abuse recovery and just about everything in between. She noted the shrink's address and clicked for directions. Visiting the office wasn't likely to get results, but it would give her a bit more leverage when she talked to her mom.

Frankie sat back, assessing the discovery. Sophia had been seeing a psychologist for years. One more skeleton lurking in her mother's closet. Did it have any bearing on the statement she'd written to ensure that General Leone was convicted of treason? Every step forward led to two sideways and one back.

Why would her mother see a psychologist? The little girl inside Frankie wanted to deny her parents had dealt with marital trouble. They'd rarely fought and as far back as she could remember they'd always been close. Marital problems didn't explain why Sophia was still keeping the appointments.

Frankie's agenda app on her computer chimed with an alert for the afternoon meeting. Grabbing her company tablet, she headed for the conference room. The meeting was a simple status update on current antivirus and malware solutions. When asked, Frankie shared an update on recent cyber crimes and the latest scam alerts she'd gathered.

She listened, watching as Sophia took notes by hand, asked questions, then moved along to the next topic. It was a rare glimpse of her in full business mode.

"Thanks, everyone," her mom finally said, flipping her notebook closed. "Keep up the great work."

Frankie caught her eye as the others filed out of the room. "One more thing, if you have just a minute?"

"Sure." Sophia gave her bright, happy smile. "You seem to have a handle on the job."

"It's great," Frankie said. "I was curious about our association with medical and mental health providers. Do we have products or programs to assist them?"

"We do," Sophia replied, unfazed. "Is there a particular area of concern?"

Frankie wanted to believe the doctor was a client now, but she'd seen the emails. "No." She swallowed. Why did she feel so terrible lying to her mom, when Sophia never told the truth? "I was just curious about the potential within the market," she said. "I have a few contacts that could benefit from our encryption products."

"Go on and talk it over with Sales if you have some ideas," Sophia said.

"Now? On my own?" Frankie wondered how her mom would slip out of this.

Sophia gave her an odd look. "I'd go with you, but I have another appointment. You can manage." She started for the door, only to turn back. "Did you and Aidan decide on a venue for the reception while you were at lunch?"

Frankie felt as though she was caught in a never-ending game of hide-and-seek. "No." She almost admitted he hadn't brought it up.

"Oh. That's fine. It will depend on the timing of the ceremony, too. We'll talk later tonight, okay?"

"Sure." Dread slithered between her shoulder blades as Sophia walked out.

Frankie didn't want to think of reception venues or anything else, and not just because this engagement was a farce. When she found the right guy and decided to marry, they were going to do it right and elope. It wasn't as if her dad was around to give her away, and she wouldn't want her wedding day shadowed by the secrets and lies her mother carried around.

Weddings were supposed to be celebrations of love, not burdened with bitterness and emotional baggage.

AIDAN WORRIED ABOUT Frankie the rest of the day. It was clear her patience was gone, and he used every spare minute of his afternoon to do the research that would give her the answers she needed. The pain and confusion in her eyes bothered him as much as the sharp glint of determination. The woman was drawn as tight as a bowstring and last night's attack put him right there with her. He didn't believe the mugging was random. They'd managed to threaten someone, but who and how?

Trusting his gut instincts, he used his phone and booked a hotel room under a different name. After work they could buy her a new phone and get checked in. They wouldn't spend the night—that would be too much temptation—but they could talk without fear of being overheard. He'd make sure they each had a key in case either of them needed an escape hatch.

With only a half hour left in the workday, he

sat down at his desk to address reports and office email, and to continue his research on his real case.

He proceeded carefully, knowing he garnered more attention from both partners because he was the fiancé rather than a typical new hire. He and Victoria had been exchanging emails since he left Chicago. She was searching for the mysterious man who'd pointed Frankie to the safe-deposit box, and Aidan was digging into Leo Solutions and their clients. Someone close to the Leone family had motive enough to embarrass and destroy them. The more he studied General Leone's service record, the more the treason charge baffled him. It felt like a smoke screen for something else. The more time he spent around Sophia, the more convinced he was she and Frankie had been used, as well.

Frankie had seen her father at Bagram, when Sophia was sure he'd been in Kabul. Sophia had claimed responsibility at the graveside, but the statement without more support was meaningless, though Aidan had passed all that on in his daily reports to Victoria.

Hearing the soft click of heels in the hallway, he wasn't surprised when Sophia stopped at his open door. "Can I bother you a minute?"

Hitting the screen saver on his computer monitor, he pushed to his feet. "Two visits in one day. I'm honored." He waited until she sat down before he did the same.

Her lips didn't quite smile. The expression reminded him of Frankie when she was trying too hard to pretend everything was fine. "I really don't want to cross a line here." She worried the edges of the folder in her hands.

"Is something wrong?"

"No." Her eyes went wide as she shook her head. "Nothing like that. It's actually not about work."

*The wedding.* Either she wasn't pestering Frankie about the details, or Frankie wasn't sharing with him. Aidan's money was on the latter.

"September will sneak up on us if we let it. We need to make some decisions quickly."

Aidan tried to sympathize with Sophia's urgency. She didn't know he'd be walking out of her life soon. "I didn't realize I'd have quite this much say in the process. My buddies teased me that it would be all bride all the time."

"With a normal bride it is," she assured him. "Frankie is...different."

Aidan smiled. "I know." He made a mental note to talk to Frankie about picking up the slack on the happy bride stuff.

Sophia's shoulders relaxed. "She doesn't say much about your side of the family."

"What don't you know from the background checks?" He kept it light, but the query was serious.

"Not that. We have all the time in the world to get to know them. I'm referring to the guest list." She handed him the folder. "This is a short list of venues in the area. I can't move forward until I have an idea of how many guests we're expecting."

*Venues? Guests?* Stuck, his skin prickled at the back of his neck. The best course on any undercover job was to keep it as true as possible. "I'm not sure any of my family will make the trip."

Sophia pursed her lips, concern in her brown eyes. "I worry about you."

He laughed that off. "Frankie and you are all the family I'll need on my wedding day." It sounded true enough when he said it out loud. He grabbed his pen, just to give himself a distraction.

"You say that now." She took a deep breath and crossed her ankles. "Yes, the wedding is about you and Frankie, but your family should be there to celebrate with you."

"I appreciate your concern," he said. "I'd planned to pay for the video and photographer."

"This isn't about who pays which bill," Sophia said with a flash of impatience. That was going around today. "We have the tech to stream it live, but it's not the same."

"My family isn't as close as yours," he began as a cloud fell over Sophia's face. Now he was concerned about two Leone women. Sophia didn't typically show this kind of agitation.

"I'm not pushing this because I want you to fit some perfect mold or expectation," she said. "I don't want you to have regrets."

*Too late.* He wasn't sure mother and daughter would overcome the pressure this engagement stunt would put on their fragile relationship when the truth came out. From his vantage point, it seemed Frankie and Sophia wanted the same things from each other: love, trust and respect.

The love was there, under the anger and pain. Although Frankie would vehemently deny it, the respect was there, too. All they needed was the trust. That would take time and practice, assuming this didn't shatter them.

"Honestly, I've never given much thought to who would be at my wedding," he said.

"You're a man," Sophia said with a wistful smile. "Frank and I basically eloped. My parents were furious with me for a time and I always regretted upsetting them. Years later, I wondered if a longer engagement might've been smart."

"Frankie told me you had to hurry things along because of his orders."

Sophia's smile brightened, transforming her face to that of a young woman in love. "That was the least of it. We were impatient to get real life started."

"We could've eloped," he pointed out. "But Frankie wanted to tell you first. She wanted to reconnect with you."

Sophia studied him, her mouth tipped up in a wry smirk. "I imagine you exerted influence over that choice."

He shrugged. "Maybe just a little."

"It only underscores my concern about having your family here. Is there something I could do or say to help?"

"No, thank you." At this rate he'd be forced to explain the situation to his parents, without blowing the case. "I'll reach out," he said, recognizing an unwinnable argument. Creative problem solving was supposedly one of his strengths, though it didn't feel like it right now.

"Thank you. I know I'm pushing, but…"

"No worries," he assured her. "I know you want what's best for Frankie."

"And you," Sophia said suddenly. "I'm sure I sound like a romantic fool, but I see how you look at each other. It's love. Your family should be able to see that love, too, especially on your wedding day."

Leaving that hanging in the air, she walked out, and he stared at the empty doorway for far too long. How exactly did Frankie look at him? He'd thought this was one-sided. Was she being convinced by the charade, too?

He thought about the way she responded to his kisses, the way her hand gripped his whenever they were together. The woman, tougher than anyone he knew, had a vulnerable side he instinctively wanted to shelter. Her search for the truth had become his cause. For her, he wanted go above and beyond the resolution of a challenging case.

There had to be a way to survive this tightrope he was walking. Any misstep could be his last and Aidan feared he wouldn't survive the fall.

He plucked the reception venue file off his desk and shoved it into his duffel bag. Refreshing his monitor, he returned to the task of gathering intel for Victoria. His new boss was the best in the private investigations business for a reason. After reviewing his last update, she'd pointed him in a new direction: the applicants who'd been *rejected* by Leo Solutions. Neither Aidan nor Victoria trusted the man who'd contacted Frankie in Savannah. They both suspected he was connected to the person behind this mess.

Due to the nature of the work at Leo Solutions, every application was screened and kept on file for reference. In a fortunate break, he discovered the rejected résumés weren't locked up behind firewalls like the personnel files of those who landed jobs. Aidan made swift work of it, wanting to get in and out without leaving a trace or raising suspicions. He had an excuse ready, but better all around if he didn't have to use it.

At last he found the man who'd approached Frankie, and gave a mental fist pump. Reading the résumé, he wondered why John Lennox hadn't made the cut. He was a little older, but his military background, three tours in the Middle East and his fitness should've made him an automatic hire. Aidan frowned, downloading the data and notes from the man's interviews with both Paul and Sophia to his flash drive.

If the dates on the dossier were accurate, Lennox's overseas service had coincided with General Leone's on all three deployments. Immediately, Aidan's thoughts turned to Frankie and her likely interpretation of this news. She'd find a way to twist the interview and no-hire into her mother's prejudice against applicants who'd known her father.

Aidan's instincts were once more prickling as he read through Paul's vague post-interview notes on Lennox. Aidan cross-referenced the email address and searched through the corporate accounts, coming up empty. It was too co-incidental to ignore.

He leaned back until his chair creaked. As an investigator, he would pass the intel on to his boss and keep Frankie out of it. Victoria would use her assets to follow up and track down this guy who seemed to know everything about Frankie's parents' histories. Still, the idea of hiding this from her made Aidan's gut twist.

"It doesn't add up," he muttered, after reading through the file again. The items Frankie had found were too personal, too specific. General Leone might've opened the account and rented the box, but it had to be Paul or Sophia who used it to get Frankie back to Seattle.

Which of them had stocked that safe-deposit box and given Lennox the key to pass on to her?

Aidan could make a case for Sophia; the woman knew only a serious catalyst would break Frankie's stubborn streak. But why paint herself so negatively in the process?

Considering Paul as a suspect had Aidan asking the same questions about making Sophia look bad. On top of that, he couldn't see what

Paul gained by undermining the face of Leo Solutions on a professional or personal level.

Aidan copied the new intel to the cloud where Victoria could access it, then ejected the drive and tucked it into his pocket. If he shared it with Frankie, Victoria had cause to fire him. If he didn't, Frankie would never trust him. The obvious answer was career above client.

Could he live with that?

*No.* The answer tolled like a church bell in his head. It didn't matter that he and Frankie were playing at romance for the sole purpose of the case. Handling this incorrectly could destroy his career. It hit him like a roundhouse kick. As his dad often said, there was always work for a man willing to get his hands dirty.

Frankie mattered more. Damn it, he'd fallen for her. Handling *her* incorrectly could destroy him, along with his heart, his sense of self and his decency. If he kept her out of it, he had no hope of exploring a real relationship with her when they resolved this case.

He couldn't live with that. Couldn't accept a result that killed any chance he had with the one woman who challenged and captivated him so thoroughly. Frankie was in the fight of her life and he wanted to be sure she never had cause to consider him an enemy.

Decision made, he set up a secondary cloud

account. He created a username and password for Frankie and uploaded the Lennox file, just in case something happened to him or the drive. Once they were done here for the day, she could take a look and they could discuss the possible ramifications over dinner out.

If he was lucky, this would be enough to make her listen to an alternate theory, though he knew it would be an uphill battle.

Everything worthwhile took effort and risk. In Frankie's case, Aidan knew the reward, gaining her trust and a chance to be with her for the long run, would be priceless.

# Chapter Ten

7:55 p.m.

For the first time, Frankie believed they would figure this out. She had a new cell phone and a key card for an "in case of emergency" hotel room near the airport, and Aidan had identified her father's friend as John Lennox. Now they just had to connect a few more dots and she could confront her mother.

She could feel the weight easing off her.

After work, Aidan had managed to lose the team tailing them, giving them space and time to relax in the hotel room. Wisely, they'd worked on the case and managed to keep their hands and lips off each other. Over Chinese takeout they'd debated the significance of the psychologist, if her father had indeed asked Lennox to take action in the event of his death, or if Lennox was being controlled by someone else.

Having returned to the performance required of them at the corporate apartment, she decided progress was a beautiful thing. Even the small steps, she thought as she sent him a text message that she was back from her bakery run and headed upstairs. It bothered her that they couldn't just pull the trigger now. What they'd found, revealed in the right way, could spell the end of Leo Solutions and leave her mother with no choice but to cooperate. If Frankie couldn't get justice for her father, maybe she'd finally get answers for her peace of mind.

She punched the call button for the elevator and tapped her phone on her palm while she waited. One second she felt absolutely certain about taking definitive action. About ruining her mother and the company. But before the next second could tick by, her resolve wavered. It seemed Aidan's warnings about family, lies and love were sinking in.

She stepped into the elevator and pressed the button for the apartment floor.

She'd been out for vengeance, if not exactly blood, ever since her father's disgrace and death. Would taking action, even righteous action, against her mother make her a hero or lump her into the category of another problem? Aidan had told her point-blank she'd be devastated if she tore her mother's professional life apart. Then again, his mom hadn't turned on his dad.

The elevator screeched and jerked to a stop, tossing Frankie down hard into a corner. She swore as the bakery bag fell and the emergency lights came on.

From her knees, she hit the red button to call for help. The emergency alarm sounded, but the elevator car jerked and dropped again. Moving slowly, she reached for her phone and checked the signal. Hopefully her text to Aidan would get out. Slinging her purse strap across her body, she pushed herself to her feet and tried to pry open the doors.

Her fingers pinched and cramped, her back ached from the effort and her shoulders burned, but the doors didn't part. "Damn it." She shook the tension out of her arms and tried again. Another screech of metal on metal sounded in the elevator shaft above her and the car tipped to the side like a sinking boat.

"Hey, lady! Can you hear me?"

Frankie followed the sound of the voice to the speaker in the instrument panel and then glanced up toward the security camera in the corner. She gave the camera lens a thumbs-up.

"Fire department is on the way. Just sit tight."

She didn't like it, but she didn't have much choice. She nodded and tried to breathe. Tight spaces weren't a big problem for her. Feeling helpless was her big hang-up and it had only become more pronounced following her injury. She fisted and stretched her fingers while she waited for the sound of sirens. It had to be her imagination, but even that small motion of her hands seemed to set the car swaying.

Determined to help herself, she looked for the service panel in the ceiling. There had to be some way out of here.

She heard a soft thud on the roof of the elevator. "Who's there?" No one answered. Whatever had landed wasn't heavy enough to cause the car to move, so she assumed it wasn't a rescue team.

But the pop and hiss, followed by a sizzle and puff of white smoke, startled her. "What the hell?" She didn't think the person monitoring the security camera could see the problem yet.

She waved her arms in front of the camera. "Hey! Help me! There's smoke or something—"

A chunk of the ceiling dropped into the elevator with her, and the smoke filled the small space with a stinging vapor and noxious odor. Her eyes watered and she covered her mouth and nose with the collar of her T-shirt.

She scrambled for the door, pulling and prying with all her might, ignoring how the car swayed with her efforts. She pounded the sleek paneling with her fists.

The voice on the other end of the intercom faded to static and she felt the gas taking effect. Thick gray smoke made her feet invisible and billowed up toward her knees. If she was meant to die here, she refused to go without a fight.

Using the railing on the back panel of the car as a toehold, she smeared the lens of the security camera with lip gloss. Then she popped open the emergency access in the ceiling. She wasn't sure what she'd do once she was in the elevator shaft, but as the smoke continued to build up, she knew she couldn't stay here.

The cleaner air in the elevator shaft cleared her head some as she pulled and wriggled her way to the roof. Looking around, she noted her slim-to-none options as the car swayed under her feet. She recognized the smell of a military-grade explosive and saw the frayed cable straining against the weight of the car. Someone had rigged this elevator and waited for the right moment to send it plummeting to the ground.

She used the flashlight on her phone to get her bearings in the dim, cavernous space, looking for the best path out. The cable creaked again and if she didn't move quickly, the saboteur would win and she'd wind up a smudge amid the debris.

Calculating the distance between her perch and the service ladder bolted to the wall between the runs, she thought she could get there. If she didn't fall, she'd climb up to the next floor and pry open those doors. The other option would be climbing down to the bottom of the shaft. With no alternative, she put away her phone and moved as cautiously as possible toward the safety of the ladder, using the cables and wiring for balance.

Light suddenly flooded the shaft and she peered up.

"Frankie?"

*Aidan!* "I'm here." Her voice was raspy from the smoke. "The elevator cable blew. Gas grenade, too."

He swore as he flashed a beam of light around the elevator shaft. "Get to the ladder."

"That's the plan," she replied.

"Faster," he said, his voice low and urgent. "There's another charge on a timer."

How had she missed it? It didn't matter. She stretched for the ladder. The cable creaked; the car shifted away. She waited until it steadied, then, using a cluster of wiring, pulled herself close enough to make the jump for the ladder. The cable creaked again as the car swung away.

"Hurry, Frankie." Aidan was lying in the open doorway, his arm stretching down to her.

She kept her eyes on his face, on the light behind him as she climbed. One rung at a time, she focused on him, rather than the dark narrow elevator shaft lit with emergency glow strips.

Finally her hand met his, wrapping around his wrist, and his strength made the last few steps easier.

Beneath her, another pop sounded, then the rasp and whip of the cable, followed by the scream of metal as the car plummeted down the shaft.

Aidan jerked her up into the brightly lit hallway as the crash swelled from fourteen stories below. Frankie trembled under his sheltering body as the explosion roared up the elevator shaft.

"Good Lord," she whispered into his chest. "I knew we were on the right track." A shiver rattled her body. "She tried to kill me." *Her mother wanted her dead.* The raw awareness was more of a shock than the attack.

"We're getting out of here," Aidan said. "No cops." He rolled to his feet, bringing her with him. "No statements." He gave her a hard look. "And no arguing."

She nodded. They were in and out of the apartment with essential gear in less than five minutes. Her back and hip protested, but she'd deal with that later. She let Aidan lead, following him up the stairs to the next floor, down the hall and into another stairwell. He pulled out a device that looked like a key fob and pressed the button.

"Signal jammer?"

He nodded. "Should mix up the building surveillance, too, if we're lucky."

Having scoped out the egress options after they'd accepted the corporate apartment, they needed only a few minutes' head start to disappear into the city. Aidan had his gun drawn and cleared each landing until they were all the way down and outside.

At street level they deftly avoided the police and fire departments. Several blocks away, he hailed a cab.

"Airport," he said, his voice gruff.

Frankie slid onto the seat beside him. "We can't leave," she said. They were too close to the goal. If they gave up now, she might never have another chance. And after that near miss, she refused to let anyone off the hook. "You realize—"

He shot her a quelling glance, his eyes harder than his voice had been.

Apparently the "no argument" rule hadn't been lifted yet. Fine. The silence gave her plenty of time to calm down so she could state her case in a way that left him no room to argue with *her*.

AIDAN WANTED TO hold her and never let go. He wanted to know she was safe, that her back was fine, but those questions would wait. If he touched her now, he'd lose his mind. He forced himself to assess their surroundings as the cab inched by the chaos in front of the building they'd just escaped. There was a killer on the loose, likely watching the result of his handiwork.

Unbidden, the image of Frankie on top of the lift filled Aidan's vision and his heart slammed against his rib cage. He'd nearly lost her. Mere seconds had separated her from certain death. Even if she hadn't fallen, she would've been wiped out by the explosion.

He pinched the bridge of his nose as the cabbie hit the freeway. In ten minutes they'd be safe in a hotel. In under an hour they could be out of the state or even the country. Not that Aidan would ever convince her to leave. She didn't have her answers yet.

For the first time since he'd taken the case, he considered cornering Sophia and forcing the issue. Not smart. Not professional.

He felt the soft touch of Frankie's hand and watched her lace her fingers through his. She gave a gentle squeeze. He could barely swallow through the lump in his throat. He rubbed the band of her engagement ring with his thumb, a welcome reminder that she'd survived. They were out of danger. For how long?

The question iced his skin. They weren't dealing with speculation or theory anymore. Something they'd discovered was making someone very nervous. The next strike was inevitable and he needed to be prepared.

"I have to report this," he said, so only she would hear him.

"Yes."

Her agreement startled him. He told the cabbie to drive through the departure area for the next group of airlines, then on to the circuit of hotels nearby.

Satisfied they hadn't been tailed, he directed the driver to stop at the next major chain. He wasn't going to expose their escape hatch just yet. He paid the fare and, with his arm at Frankie's waist, moved directly to the check-in desk. He used a false ID and credit card, requesting a room on the first floor. He felt her watching him, but there was no way in hell he could deal with an elevator right now.

He didn't care that it was irrational, only cared about keeping her alive.

They reached the room, and the moment he'd locked the door, his patience evaporated. He dropped the bags and wrapped his arms around her. Holding her close, his hands splayed across her back, he measured every breath. She was alive. In his arms.

He released her long enough to move their gear to the bed and pull the curtains closed. When he turned back to her, she hadn't moved. He hugged her again, tucking her head to his shoulder. "I was terrified," he confessed.

"Aidan."

"Don't ask me to let go." He couldn't do it, not yet. His palm moved up and down her spine, lingering too long at her lower back.

"I'm fine," she said. Her hands slid under his jacket and fisted in his shirt. "I promise. Thank you for saving me."

"You had it under control." He moved just enough to tip up her chin and lay a soft kiss on her lips. Managing to push back the panic and terror, he knew the dam wouldn't hold for long. She was alive and well. He might remember that for all of five minutes without a touch or word, but he didn't want to chance it. He smoothed a loose tendril of her hair behind her ear. "I was just moral support."

"More than that," she whispered, gazing up at him, her eyes shining with a rush of need that matched his. She pushed her fingers into his hair and brought his mouth back to hers. Her lips parted with a sigh and his tongue swept inside, tangled with hers.

The abrasive odors of oil and machinery, explosives and the smoke grenade, clung to her hair. Her taste, sweet as honey and warm as a summer day, overwhelmed his other senses. He needed her. All of her. He needed to take her into himself and keep her safe. Always. He didn't want to think how impossible that was.

There was nothing of comfort or reassurance in this blatant mating of mouths, no simple curiosity of attraction. This kiss was full of need hemmed on all sides by sheer desperation. He'd nearly lost her before he had a chance to tell her how much she meant to him.

His hands spanned her trim waist, moved higher so her breasts filled his palms. He tweaked the hard tips through her shirt and she arched into his touch. Gripping her backside, he brought her hips close, pressing her against his erection. He bent his head and explored the softness of her skin, down the column of her throat and back up to her ear. "I need you."

When she trembled, whispered his name, he kissed her until they were both shaking and breathless.

He shrugged out of his jacket and reached for the hem of her shirt, pulling it up and over her head in one swift move.

Her skin glowed golden around the simple white fabric of her bra. "Francesca," he whispered across the sensitive skin of her breasts. She wasn't Frankie the client or pretend fiancée now. The case was irrelevant. The games were over. She was the woman he wanted more than his next breath. The woman he needed to give that breath meaning. His hands on her hips, he drew the stiff peak of her nipple into his mouth, teasing her through the fabric. She held him close, running her fingers through his hair, over his ears.

His hands learned her curves, the dips and hollows, in long, slow strokes from her waist across the flare of her hips.

She shoved at him and he stopped immediately. He had no time to ask what he'd done wrong, as she yanked his shirt from his waistband, gasping, "I need to touch you."

"I'm all yours." He'd never spoken words that meant as much.

FRANKIE PRESSED HER PALMS to Aidan's wide, lean chest and backed him toward the bed. She could feel the heat of him through the fabric, but she wanted skin. She pushed his shirt up and away and just stared. He was perfect. Smooth skin, hard muscle and ridges she couldn't wait to trace and taste.

Her heart was racing, and though the warning signs of stress were firing in her back, she was done with foreplay. She wouldn't be denied this moment. The twinges only served as a reminder of how fleeting life was. She'd survived an IED, paralysis, and now a sabotaged elevator. She deserved a little happiness and positive adrenaline. Just to change it up.

She flicked open the button of his jeans, eased the zipper down until she could wrap her hand around his thick erection. Her breath caught in her chest, her pulse throbbing in her ears at the feel of him. So close and yet not nearly close enough.

Moving in a passionate frenzy around and between searing kisses, they shed his interfering clothing until at last he stretched out on the bed, drawing her down beside him. She wanted him fast and hard. The slow and tender could wait. She needed him to hurry and blot out the terror crowding her, to affirm her survival.

She hesitated. In the midst of crawling over his amazing body, she froze.

The sudden bout of nerves surprised her. She hadn't been with anyone since her recovery, and she wasn't sure what might happen. Everything in her back felt normal most of the time and she didn't make a habit of expecting the worst. Sex wasn't any more rigorous than running, from a functional standpoint. She'd regained her mobility and fitness, but there was nothing she could do about the scars Aidan hadn't seen.

"Is there a problem?" He sat up, drawing her between his widespread knees. Spearing a hand into her hair, he pulled her lips to his and leveled her with another devastating kiss. "Second thoughts? Please say no."

She closed her eyes and blurted out an excuse. "No second thoughts. It's been a while, that's all."

He slid her bra straps down over her shoulders, his face so close his breath raised goose bumps on her sensitive skin. "I can't decide if that's more or less pressure on me."

She wanted to laugh, but it sputtered and died on a gasp when he unhooked her bra and took her bared breast into his mouth. "Francesca. You're beautiful."

Feeling his words more than she heard them, she decided. She'd shatter his illusions of beauty later. She leaned over to turn out the light.

"Don't." He stilled her hand. "Let me see you tonight. All of you."

"Aidan." She turned shy, an unprecedented sensation. "You don't know what you're asking." She spoke to his perfect, sculpted chest, unable to meet his eyes. "The repairs are...difficult." It was the least offensive word she could think of.

"You are perfect." He was soothing her, hypnotizing her with soft strokes over her shoulders, down her arms. "The strongest woman I know." His mouth followed, covering her, tasting her, chasing away the chill hiding in her bones. "Let me show you what I see."

She was no match for him when he looked into her eyes as he stripped away the rest of her clothes. He brought her hands to his shoulders, easing back so she practically melted on top of him, giving her the control and the choice.

"Francesca," he murmured over and over in that mesmerizing voice. His hands flowed and coaxed, erasing her scars, until she felt her body as he did.

It was like floating through a beautiful, dynamic dream as she lowered her body, taking him in carefully when she wanted to rush. He filled her so well she didn't want to move. She wanted to savor. Gently at first, she lifted her hips, testing and teasing the limits of his desire and her patience. His hands gripped her hips and he changed the rhythm to suit him. Them.

The pleasure coursed through her with every stroke, building. The climax crashed over her and she cried out as her body shuddered around him. He flexed his hips, driving deep, deeper until she couldn't discern where he ended and she began. Her body instinctively clung, gripping him tight, reluctant to let go.

When he stretched out beside her with a satisfied sigh, she curled into him, her hand resting over his heart, the light glinting off the diamond on her finger. She stared at the stone and the setting, knowing she'd given him far more than her body.

His hand traced circles over her shoulder and he pressed a kiss to the top of her hair. She'd dropped her heart into his care. Worse, she realized as exhaustion claimed her, she trusted him not to break it.

FRANKIE WOKE IN the middle of the night, knowing she wouldn't get any more sleep. There wasn't a better sign of feeling safe than the fact that they'd slept soundly. She slipped out from under Aidan's arm, turned out the light and grabbed a T-shirt and yoga pants from her suitcase on her way to the shower. At some point she was going to have to assess what they'd just done in that bed. She'd have to address how she'd left herself open to him, body and soul. Right now she locked on to the easy fib that the sex had been about reaffirming life. They'd experienced a standard biological reaction to the adrenaline spike of survival. Simple.

Under the hot pulse of the shower spray, it didn't feel simple, but she ignored the new awareness pressing in on her. The priority had to be the work. Her search for answers had gotten her mugged and nearly killed. It was past time to take a stand against her mother's schemes. Frankie toweled off, dressed and twisted her wet hair into a loose braid.

There had to be hard evidence. Without it, Aidan would continue to do his job and offer conflicting theories. She couldn't bear the idea of him siding with Sophia on any topic. Worse, she couldn't bear the small voice in her head that suggested he could be right, that her mother wasn't guilty of awful things. That was the voice of the heartbroken child inside her, not the woman smart enough to know better.

She opened her laptop, turning it away from Aidan so she wouldn't wake him while she tried to put the pieces together. Rubbing her temples, she went back to the beginning, to the treason charge, looking at every piece in light of what she and Aidan had found along the way.

It helped, Aidan's identification of Lennox, and she pushed her research skills to the limit to make the connections between Lennox and her father, her father and the supposed act of treason. He'd been at Bagram, not Kabul. A general didn't travel around unnoticed. How had her mother, an expert analyst, made such a costly mistake?

Too quickly Frankie wanted to cycle back,

pointing to the blatant lies in her mother's statement, but she fought to stay objective. For Aidan.

She stood, stretching side to side and forward, loosening tight muscles as she let her mind work. Her team had been attacked. Units under her father's command had been ambushed, the objective compromised presumably because he'd tipped off the other side for money. Her husband found guilty, Sophia had chosen to retire and start her company. Who gained from taking down the Leone family?

"Come back to bed, love."

Aidan's voice, gravelly from sleep, tempted her. She didn't want to resist. "Can't sleep." She didn't dare look at him. "I'm almost there."

Behind her she heard the mattress give as he got up. He turned on the light and denim rustled as he pulled on his jeans.

His chest was warm on her back when he wrapped his arms around her, linking his hands at her waist. "I think you're trying too hard. Let it rest."

"I'll rest when I have answers. We're running out of time."

"Your mother may not have the answers, Frankie."

The nickname rang hollow in her ears, after he'd called her Francesca when his hands and mouth were heating her body. She shivered. If he was right, what would she do? She moved back to the table, easing into the chair.

"Why do you do that?" he asked. "Sit so carefully."

"Habit. Early in the rehab my hip would catch and lock up. I would jerk or wince and everyone stared or asked about it. I learned to move so my weaknesses didn't show."

His short laughter startled her and she stared at him as he knelt beside her chair. "What weaknesses?"

She loved him for that. Kissed him for that. She wrapped his bigger hand in both of hers, needing that contact as she asked a question of her own. "Why are you so convinced Sophia is innocent in all this?"

"I've been looking at both of you, past and present, with objective eyes."

"She's fooled you," Frankie protested. "That statement—"

"If the statement is real, she gave it in good faith. The intel might've been flawed. If the document you found is fake, who put it there?" His blue eyes were steady on hers. "I'm not fooled. Not by her or you." Aidan stood and pulled Frankie up with him, his arms banding tight around her. "You're hurting. You've been robbed of everything you valued and you want a hard target to attack."

She leaned back, just enough to meet his gaze, since she didn't want him to let go. "I was a target just a few hours ago."

His face blanched. "I'm well aware." His lips brushed over her forehead, her nose, then claimed her mouth. "Despite any flaws, Sophia is a mother delighted with her daughter. Awed and inspired by you. Whatever happened, she loves you."

That only made it worse. Frankie flinched. "Take that back."

"I won't."

"That was before." Frankie felt the facts dragging her down into a well of despair. She had to *know* or walk away. Walking away was weakness. "If you're so sure it wasn't Sophia, *show* me why."

She expected him to sit at the computer, call up something he and Victoria had found. Instead, he stalked over to the duffel bag he'd brought along and unzipped the end pocket. Tossing a folder full of brochures and information onto the table, he glared at her. "Go on. Take a look."

She poked at the pile, startled by the glossy images of handsome men in tuxedos, couples lounging on a cruise ship, dancing in a class-room. "What is this?"

"Your mother keeps dropping this stuff at my desk. I can pull up the emails, too, if you'd like to read them. Questions about my preferences on tux colors, buffet or plated meals, suggestions for honeymoon destinations. Seems she's traveled extensively."

"Well, of course. The army toted us all around the world."

"Uh-huh." He planted his hands on his hips. "She's been telling me which climates you enjoyed most, which excursions and discoveries made you light up."

"What?" The behavior he was describing baffled Frankie. Everything she found pointed to a woman all too eager to ditch her past for a better venture.

Aidan pressed his hands to his eyes and she imagined he was counting to ten. Or maybe one hundred.

"Your mother *loves* you. She wouldn't be working this hard on the wedding, wouldn't be sharing the highlights of your childhood with me, if she wanted you dead."

"She's hiding something," Frankie insisted, but the argument felt flat. "Playing us."

"No." He shook his head. "We're playing her."

"That was the plan." She wagged her finger

between them. "None of this pretense would be necessary if she'd been honest with me from the start."

"Think, Frankie! She can't give you answers she doesn't have. Take another perspective and consider the possibility that she's protecting *you*."

He spoke with such conviction she wanted to believe him. "We were close once. My family was a team. Someone twisted that into lies."

He gripped her elbows, gave her a gentle shake. "You deserve answers. I know you're hurting. But your mother is too direct, too efficient to waste this much time on wedding stuff if her goal is to kill you."

Aidan drew in a big breath. "You know her better, I'll grant you that. But your history and grief are clouding your view."

He had to be wrong. Frankie couldn't see how anyone else gained from this fiasco. Who else would care if she lived or died?

"All right." Frankie sat down at her computer, ignoring the wedding paraphernalia. She motioned for him to pull up a chair. "Walk me through it. If my mom's just a patsy, let's find the culprit."

# Chapter Eleven

*Wednesday, April 13, 7:50 a.m.*

Frankie and Aidan arrived at work hand in hand, parting ways with a quick kiss in the lobby. They'd made this their routine from the start, but today it felt different. More real, far more significant.

It didn't take any investigation to know making love with Aidan changed her, she thought, taking the stairs up to her floor. Love? No. Her mind backpedaled in denial. It was excellent sex that left her feeling soft and mushy all over. Something in the way Aidan had touched her reached her heart, yes. The experience had definitely surpassed her expectations. Still, it was too soon to burden either of them with *love*.

She tugged open the stairwell door, refusing to dwell on the conversation she'd overheard, instead greeting the others on her floor as she hurried to her office.

At least she and Aidan had solid indications her mother had been involved, if not willingly, with her dad's downfall. As Aidan had reviewed the facts, Frankie had grudgingly admitted he was right. Everything she pointed to was circumstantial, some of it possibly fabricated. If they could just prove it, they could move on. She wished she knew what that next phase of her life would look like.

Frankie dropped her purse into her desk drawer and locked it. Booting up her computer, she thought about what Aidan had asked her to look for today while she pretended to analyze company data looking for criminal trends, security options and new clients to approach.

It still surprised her how much she enjoyed the work that was supposed to be short-term cover. If they didn't find something by the end of the week, she'd have to resign her post at the police station and stick this out, or else leave her mom in the lurch. Somehow the idea wasn't as appealing as it had been forty-eight hours ago.

Frankie closed her eyes and leaned back in her chair. She sure as hell never expected to carry away any guilt over what had to be done in her effort to clear her father's name.

At the sound of a soft rap on her office door, she sat up, her eyes popping open.

"Good morning," her mother said, peeking around the door. "Late night?"

Either her mother was diabolical, a theory Aidan dismissed, or her surveillance team had no idea someone had tried to kill her daughter last night. Frankie heard Aidan's voice urging her to play nice. "Hi, Mom. I just didn't sleep well."

"Wedding plans do that to a bride."

Frankie struggled to maintain the eye contact. "I suppose."

"Was it the elevator? I heard there was an emergency call with an elevator in your building. Do we need to move you and Aidan?"

"Some kind of mechanical failure," Frankie said slowly. Her mother had friends tailing them who'd surely seen the emergency personnel. If she was responsible for the bugs in the apartment, too, did she know the two of them had been gone all night? Frankie needed another cup of tea before tackling these mental gymnastics. "Don't worry about us."

"Okay. You know—" Sophia took a small step inside the office "—before your father and I rushed our wedding, the most fun we had was cake testing."

Frankie swallowed. It wasn't just the idea of

cake at eight o'clock in the morning. It was the image of her parents' loving, romantic relationship spiraling into something so terrible. Did love ever last? Great, now she had one more impossible question in need of an answer. "I remember you made chocolate cake every time he returned from a deployment or business trip."

"His aunt Josie baked the cake for the reception my parents hosted and she gave me the recipe," Sophia said. "Does Aidan like chocolate cake?"

Frankie nodded, hoping it was true.

"I'll email you the recipe."

"Thanks." Frankie deliberately turned her attention to her computer monitor.

Sophia ignored the hint to leave. "I don't want to step on any toes," she said, her hands clasped tight around the travel mug of coffee in her hands. "But I, um, made a few calls and if you'd like we can preview some bakers this afternoon."

"What?"

"Just to streamline the process," she said with a tentative smile. "Naturally you and Aidan will want to make the final choice together."

"Mom." Frankie was appalled at the soft sound of her own voice. The love shining in her mother's gaze was worse. Aidan was right, this wasn't the face of a woman who wanted to destroy her daughter.

Frankie cleared her throat and reminded herself she had nothing to lose by playing along with wedding plans that wouldn't happen. It didn't help. She was in too deep with her mom and the fake fiancé who'd become her real lover. "That's thoughtful. Thanks."

"I sifted through the recommendations and reviews and chose bakers who still had openings in September."

It was such a caring-mother move. Frankie managed to get air in and out of her lungs without choking. The misery over what had begun as a white lie mounted. Worse, this morning it was surprisingly easy to imagine exchanging vows with Aidan. She gave herself a mental kick. They were here for a purpose and she was letting herself get carried away by the game.

Sophia caught her lip between her teeth. "Are you angry?"

"No." Not the way she had been. "It just sort of hit me that we do need to make plans. I'd thought I'd have time to enjoy being engaged."

"And you should." Her mother sank gracefully into a chair. "We can always shift the date."

"Maybe." Frankie mustered a smile. "I'll

probably want to move it up after we meet with the bakers."

The tension fled from Sophia's face. "Oh, good. Afterward maybe you and I can have dinner down in Pike Place Market."

"That would be great, Mom." If a mother-daughter dinner worked, she wouldn't squander the opportunity.

Sophia's phone chimed from her pocket. "Meeting alarm," she said. "It's so hard to think business when my daughter is getting married!"

Frankie admired her mother's ability to hurry without a single outward sign of stress. Years of maintaining her composure as the general's wife had been good training. It should serve as a warning that Sophia Leone was capable of saying one thing while doing another.

Thanks to Aidan planting doubts in her mind, Frankie no longer believed her mother could book wedding cake tasting after ordering a hit on her only child.

Frankie dug into the work. It was the only way to get her mind off the not-going-to-happen wedding plans. She even gave the cyber-crime trends her full attention for over an hour before turning her focus back to her quest for the truth, coming up empty again. She swore under her breath. Either her mother had disposed of all evidence or, as Aidan and Victoria would happily point out, Sophia was innocent. Frankie needed to find something soon. Victoria wouldn't let her monopolize a Colby investigator indefinitely.

"Think!" She drummed her fingertips on her desktop as she considered her next move. There had to be some confirmation of Sophia's source, or a trace of her obligations at the time of the operation that ended Frank Leone's military career.

Frankie worked her way through the company directory, focusing on the legal and organizational angles as the company came together. How long had Sophia and Paul kicked around this idea before taking action?

And suddenly, there it was, the validation Frankie had been looking for. According to the official statement, Sophia had been consulting in Washington, DC, when Frankie was injured. So why did these travel documents show her mother and Paul traveling on a military flight from Germany to New York? Paul had then returned to Seattle, while Sophia met Frankie at Walter Reed Hospital in Maryland.

Her stomach sank. It was the proof she'd wanted to find, what she'd put all her energy into for months. Forty-eight hours ago she would've marched into her mother's office for a confrontation. Today, she saved the information for Aidan to review first. It was still a file in a database and, as he'd pointed out repeatedly, possibly manufactured.

If her mother wasn't guilty of taking down her dad, who would want to make it look that way? Frustrated, Frankie used every computer skill she possessed to catalog the information and store it securely until she and Aidan could plan the next move.

AIDAN SPENT EVERY free minute of his day working on Frankie's case. Now that he had her on his side, he didn't want to relinquish the advantage. Paul found him as he and the trainees wrapped up a session on hand-to-hand strategies. "Looks good," the older man said.

"They're coming along," Aidan agreed.

Despite the words, Aidan couldn't shake the sensation that Paul wasn't happy with anything at Leo Solutions right now. Aidan didn't have anything solid to pin that on and it made him think he was becoming as paranoid about the man as Frankie was about her mother. Still, his investigative instincts were in high gear.

Paul gestured with the phone in his hand. "Sophia tells me she set up a preview of bakeries for tonight. Says she and Frankie need some time to narrow down the style and choices before they invite you to a tasting. It's code for 'girls' night out,'" he said, looking less than happy.

"All right." It required a little too much effort today to remember this was a cover story. After last night—before, if Aidan was honest with himself—he couldn't quite see his future without Frankie in it. "As long as she doesn't leave me out of everything."

"Ha!" Paul's sharp bark of laughter gave way to a rare, genuine smile. "Trust me, you'll want to leave the details to the women. The days after the ceremony are when the heavy lifting begins."

Aidan just nodded. That wasn't how he envisioned marriage, but he'd never gotten that far, so what did he know? "Thanks for the heads-up. I should get back to it." With his evening free he could spend the time digging into the company's records for the source behind the ruination of Frankie's family.

Paul cleared his throat and managed to keep a smile in place. "How about you and I head to my club for dinner? There's a weekly card game if you're interested."

"Sounds great." Anything that gave him a better glimpse of Paul could be helpful.

"I have a six o'clock meeting. Then I can swing by the apartment and pick you up by seven-thirty."

"We can leave from here," Aidan offered, seizing the excuse to stay late. "I'll have time to clean up and change clothes between classes and the paperwork."

"All right," Paul agreed. "I'll send a text when my meeting ends."

Busy man, and he liked to keep it that way, Aidan thought as Paul walked off. More accurately, he liked to make others believe he was indispensable.

Aidan wasn't convinced, no matter how Sophia explained the professional partnership. Granted, he hadn't been on-site long, but the vibe he picked up was interesting. Employees seemed utterly devoted to Sophia and wary of Paul. There had to be a reason, beyond the man's reticent nature.

Unfortunately, Aidan hadn't been on the job long enough for anyone to confide in him about specifics. And with the elevator attack, he didn't want to drag this out. He sent a text message to Frankie about his plans with Paul and then headed to the mat for the next lesson. When the classes ended, Aidan cleaned up for dinner and retreated to his desk while he waited for Paul.

It hadn't been easy worming his way past the corporate security protocols, but Aidan had experience and tenacity on his side. He'd given up the direct approach—leaving that to Frankie—

and started his investigation through lower-level personnel. As a trainer he used his access to review how each personal security officer was connected to Paul, Sophia or both. It made sense that the men and women who'd been with the company since the outset had worked with one or both of them on other endeavors.

He found his way back to the Lennox file and continued searching for the man who'd approached Frankie in Savannah. The guy couldn't just show up and disappear. Aidan had just found a plane ticket matching Lennox's ID when the text message from Paul came through.

At least he had something to chew on as soon as dinner was over. Quickly, Aidan copied the information to the cloud storage sites for Victoria. He'd tell Frankie in person, hopefully over wedding cake samples.

Paul was uncharacteristically chatty in the car and Aidan struggled to keep up with the conversation while his mind worked through the case.

"Scotch?" Paul offered, pulling down a panel of the backseat to reveal two highball glasses and a decanter of pale amber liquid.

"I'll pass," Aidan replied. "Thanks."

"Suit yourself." He poured a generous serving into one glass. "Has to be the best perk of having a driver in this city," he said.

"You're not from Seattle?"

"Hell, no." He sipped the Scotch. "I tried to convince Sophia there were areas more conducive to our business, but she was determined to pin the headquarters here." He gazed about, eyeing the traffic through the windows.

They had plenty of time to enjoy the view of Seattle sparkling at twilight at the edge of Puget Sound, since the freeway was clogged with commuters. As traffic jams went, this wasn't bad. This part of the world was so different from his other experiences, Aidan soaked it up.

Paul raised his glass, draining the contents. "So, how are things going?"

"Well, thanks," Aidan replied honestly. "It's good work—"

A car rear-ended the sedan, cutting him off.

"What was that?" Paul demanded, twisting around in his seat.

His pulse jumping into high gear, Aidan looked in turn. A bullet screamed through the rear window, exiting through the windshield. Aidan hunkered down, resisting the urge to go for the weapon in his ankle holster.

"Get us out of here," Paul roared to the driver.

The man jerked the wheel and slammed his hand on the horn as he aimed for the left shoulder, searching for any opening on the crowded roadway. The acrid odor of burning rubber tinged the air when he gunned the engine through tight spaces. The car that hit them gave pursuit. Aidan and Paul were tossed back into the seat and then side to side as the driver evaded within his limited options.

"Where's a cop when you need one?" Paul grumbled. Keeping his head low, he managed to get the glassware back into the console and tuck the liquor station away.

Aidan muttered something agreeable as he mentally weighed his limited options. He hoped Frankie and Sophia weren't experiencing a similar attack.

Paul's driver cut across traffic from the left shoulder, aiming for the next exit. Aidan couldn't understand the decision. The surface streets would give the maniac behind them better access as they jerked in a stop-and-go pattern between lanes.

Bullets started to fly again. One after another struck the window closest to Aidan, creating spiderweb patterns in the glass. He ducked down, taking Paul with him. "Are you hit?"

"No," the older man said. "What about you?"

"I'm good." Aidan pulled a pen from his sport coat and wrote down the plate number of the car that had hit them. "Got the license," he muttered.

Paul gave him a small smile. "Good job."

"We're clear, boss," the driver said.

Aidan followed Paul's lead, resuming his place in the backseat as they merged with traffic exiting the freeway. "What now?" he asked.

The remnants of the rear window exploded and Paul's answer was swallowed by a spray of sparkling glass and a violent oath. Aidan felt a burning in his back and across his arm as a wet warmth seeped slowly down his side. The coppery tang of blood filled his nostrils. "I'm hit." Had he managed to get the words out or had he only thought them?

It was his first gunshot wound and he hadn't expected it to make him woozy. He didn't understand how the shot was even possible until he looked back over his shoulder and caught the movement of a sniper on the overpass above and behind them.

He'd been set up, he thought, afraid this time he had said it aloud. "Hospital," he rasped, reaching for his phone.

Paul shouted orders to the driver while applying pressure to Aidan's back.

Aidan reached into his pocket, relieved his phone was in one piece. He pulled up Frankie's contact page.

"What are you doing?" Paul demanded.

The call went to voice mail. The sound of the greeting Frankie had recorded on her new phone made him feel better immediately.

"Fr-Frankie," Aidan stammered. "Baby," he said, using the code word for trouble. "Got shot." It was only a small fib, not an outright lie. "Here's Paul."

He handed over the phone. "Tell her what hospital."

He listened as Paul explained where they were headed, and then he reclaimed his phone.

"I'll call Sophia as soon as we get to the ER," Paul assured him. "Just in case they don't get the voice mail."

"Good." Aidan let his head drop back onto the seat, hoping that didn't make him a better target. The wind rushed through the destroyed rear window, the sound and chill keeping him awake as the driver sped to the nearest hospital.

It felt like a small eternity before the car stopped. Aidan was soon surrounded by people in scrubs helping him from the vehicle. He heard Paul explain they'd been attacked on the freeway and then, finally, he heard nothing more than the orders of medical staff around him.

"It's not that bad," he murmured as they cut away his clothing. "I need my phone."

A nurse argued with him, but he had to tell Victoria. "Aidan Abbot, Interpol," he said, hoping they wouldn't ask for official ID. "I need five seconds to send a text, and then you can have at it."

Over the gurney a doctor exchanged a look and a shrug with the nurse. The woman handed him his phone and he managed to send the text. Victoria would know what to do next. "Thank you," he said. His head was swimming again, just from that small effort. "What the hell happened to my head?"

His questions went unanswered as the medical team worked to assess and address his injuries. At least he was out of Paul's reach for the moment. Assuming that bastard was behind the whole mess.

More important, if he didn't survive this, the Colby Agency would protect Frankie and could flush out the mole inside Leo Solutions.

## Chapter Twelve

Frankie was completely overwhelmed and more than a little worried when her mother drove out to a small, private airfield on the west side. "We're flying to interview bakers?"

Sophia chuckled and reached across the console to pat Frankie's knee. "No. I just needed neutral territory to bring them all together. A friend of mine let me use the conference room here. And I didn't want any distractions from the office."

Frankie was distracted enough with all the details and emotions she could barely fit into the box in the corner of her mind. This woman didn't reconcile with the distant widow Frankie remembered after her dad's suicide. She was much closer to the vibrant, reliable mother from Frankie's childhood. "You didn't have to do this," she said, her guilt riding heavy on her shoulders.

"I want to. You're going to marry a wonderful man and your wedding should be perfect from start to finish."

Only in her dreams, Frankie thought. "You barely know him."

"I know you," Sophia countered. "You're smart and an excellent judge of character. If he wasn't worthy, you never would've said yes when he proposed."

Frankie knew that no matter how delicious the presentation, she would taste only bitterness today. Sophia put the car in Park and wiggled her fingers. "A man who puts a ring like that on your hand is serious about forever."

Oh, God. This wedding business was way out of control.

Sophia patted her arm. "Sweetheart, you're starting a life together and I want to celebrate that moment with you to the fullest." She reached for her door handle. "Let's go eat cake!"

Frankie managed to make a sound that resembled laughter. If she was such an excellent judge of character, why did she feel that her family was one lie on top of another? She had believed her parents were in love, devoted and committed to each other and to her. She'd believed her mother had supported her dad through the accusations. Then she'd believed her mother had set him up. And now she believed, as Aidan did, that something bigger and darker had manipulated them all.

What did she know about anyone's true character? She barely recognized herself anymore, running around pretending one thing while thinking and feeling ten others.

Further self-assessment took a backseat as she walked into the conference room. Her mother had pulled out all the stops. Tables were draped in white, and seven different bakeries had created elaborate displays. "Holy cow," Frankie whispered. "Mom."

"This is fabulous," Sophia gushed, striding forward to greet the bakers. "Thank you all so much for doing this at the last minute."

Frankie marveled at the effort she had made, as well as the bakers. This had taken more than a few phone calls. Would the real Sophia Leone please stand up?

She and her mother set out to evaluate each display. They tasted two samples from each baker and flipped through presentation books of designs. Overwhelmed didn't begin to cover it. Sophia conducted a group interview of sorts and Frankie chimed in with an occasional opinion. No pricing was discussed, just options and preferences. It was clear to everyone in the room Sophia wasn't putting a limit on the wedding budget.

If Frankie could've crawled into a hole, she would have.

"If we have a family recipe for a specific cake, is that something any of you would consider? Not for the formal cake," Sophia clarified, "but for a groom's cake or a honeymoon suite surprise. I don't want my daughter or me worried about baking on the day of, you understand."

That generated more favorable responses and Frankie found herself as enamored as the bakers by Sophia's bright, happy smile.

Her phone vibrated in her pocket and she checked the display, irrationally hoping it was Aidan. Seeing that she'd missed a call from his number, she excused herself to listen to the voice mail.

He stammered her name, sounding drunk.

Her heart lunged into her throat.

"Baby." Hearing the code word for trouble, Frankie rapped on the glass window to get Sophia's attention. "Got shot," Aidan's message went on.

Frankie swayed at the news. "Oh, my God!" Suddenly Paul's voice was telling her the car had been attacked on the freeway and they were headed to the hospital.

Frankie fought down a tidal wave of panic as

her mother joined her. "We have to go," she told Sophia, her hands shaking. "Aidan's been shot."

Her mom's eyes went wide. "How? Where?" She dashed back into the conference room for her purse. "He and Paul were together," she said as they ran for the car.

"Paul sounded fine," Frankie assured her through clenched teeth. She used her phone to search the news networks for any reports of a freeway sniper. No results. Either the story was too new or the attack had been focused solely on Paul and Aidan.

Sophia reached over and clutched Frankie's hand as she drove. "Paul won't let anything happen to Aidan. Just hang in there."

Frankie hoped she was right. It felt like hours rather than minutes before they reached the ER, and her heart threatened to beat out of her chest. Sophia dropped Frankie at the door and then drove off to find a parking space.

Frankie raced up to the emergency room information desk. "Aidan Abbot." She paused, the words jammed behind the panicked beating of her heart. "My fiancé. Gunshot wound."

The nurse behind the desk nodded in recognition. "He's stable. If you'll have a seat, we'll tell you more when we know something."

"I need to see him right now." A rush of tears blurred her vision. "Now," she repeated. She hadn't been this frantic since waking in that hospital bed with no feeling below her waist.

"Frankie." His hand at her elbow, Paul drew her aside.

She looked up, wiping the tears from her cheeks as he put his arm around her. Where had he come from? Why wasn't there a mark on him? Was that Aidan's blood on his jacket? Fear tore through her. She shrugged off Paul's touch and stepped out of his reach. "You did this. Somehow." She thought of the travel documents and the Lennox interview. If not Sophia, it had to be Paul pulling the strings. "You set this up."

"You're upset." The man's voice was gentle, but his eyes were cold. "Understandable. Just take a breath." His gaze slid past her and she heard high heels clicking rapidly on the tile flooring.

Frankie attacked, drilling a finger into his chest. "It's you. Last night you tried to kill me, and now him. No way I'll let you get away with this."

"Frankie," her mother said. "What's going on? How is Aidan?"

"He's stable," Paul answered before Frankie could.

"Thank God for that." Sophia pressed a hand to her chest. "What happened?"

"Road rage, I guess," he explained, without explaining anything at all. "Aidan claims he caught some of the license plate of the car. We were rear-ended and then shot at."

Sophia sucked in a breath. "Are you sure you're not hurt?" She gestured to the blood-stains on his clothes.

"I'm fine."

Frankie had calmed down enough to speak again. Though she doubted anyone would like what she had to say. "Of course he's fine. The attack was aimed at Aidan. Paul here wants us off his trail."

"You're out of your mind," Paul accused.

"I'm right." Frankie fisted her hand, eager to reach for the knife in her purse. "We've been tailed and mugged, attacked and shot at. You even bugged the apartment."

Staring at her in bewilderment, Sophia echoed, "Bugged?" She looked to Paul. "What is she talking about?"

"This is hardly the place to discuss these things," he chided, his voice low. "Your mother is the public face of a prominent security company."

"I want to see Aidan," Frankie demanded. Her mother's arms went around her, drawing her close. Frankie's first instinct was to pull away, but she simply didn't possess the wherewithal.

"He's going to be fine," Paul insisted. "The police are on their way."

"As if I'd believe anything you say." Frankie jerked out of her mother's embrace. "Either of you. I came here, we came here because—" She caught herself in the nick of time and dragged in a deep breath. "Because I thought we could be a family," she said to her mom. "It was Aidan's idea." She tried to remember more of the cover story and couldn't. She pushed her hands through her hair. "I just need to see him."

Her mother's full lips compressed to a straight line and she stalked back to the registration desk.

"How's that family idea working?" Paul stuffed his hands into his pockets. "Since you showed up with that chip on your shoulder, she's bent over backward for you and you—"

"Frankie." Sophia snapped her fingers and pointed to a nurse wearing a harried expression. "Hurry."

Frankie didn't have time to figure out what Paul meant or listen to a lecture from the sullen man. With a parting glare for him, she joined the nurse and tried to pull herself together before seeing Aidan.

She supposed it couldn't be too bad if he wasn't in surgery. Still, she'd be the one to decide if he was fine. Not Paul, standing out there without a scratch on him, lecturing her about family. Bastard.

Another nurse stepped out of the emergency treatment bay. "You're the fiancée?"

Frankie nodded. The fake fiancée dumb enough to have fallen in love with her undercover groom.

"He's been asking for you."

"Thanks." She walked through the split in the curtain and, seeing him alert and smiling, her anger and worry faded. He motioned her closer to the bed and laced his fingers with hers. *Relief* wasn't a strong enough word. He was pale, but the monitor showed steady vitals. "You're okay?"

She examined every inch she could see as the words *I love you* and *don't scare me* danced on the tip of her tongue. She wouldn't say them, not here. She couldn't put that pressure on him. It wasn't his fault she'd fallen so hard and fast.

"Stop looking for trouble," he said. "I'm fine, I promise." He raised her hand to his lips.

"Hardly fine. You're in an ER," she pointed out. "You've been shot."

He laughed a little and then winced at the resulting pain.

"Tell me what happened." She kept her voice low and bent to give him a kiss on the cheek. "Did you find something?"

He shook his head, but the gleam in his eyes told her the answer was yes. He didn't want to discuss it here.

"None of the news agencies are reporting a freeway sniper."

He grunted. "I gave the plate number to the cops who came by a few minutes ago."

"How bad is it, really?"

"I'm fine," he insisted. "It's all superficial. I got clocked behind the ear with debris and have a mild concussion. That gave me more trouble than the gunshot."

When the doctor came around an hour later to discharge him, Frankie verified that he'd left nothing out regarding his injuries and that she understood the instructions and danger signs to watch for overnight.

IT WAS NICE, in a strange way, to have Frankie fuss over him. To watch her dark, expressive eyes fill with relief when he finally convinced her the bullet had done little more than graze him. He had a few stitches, and thanks to the concussion he was bordering on exhausted by the time they convinced her mother he was fine and escaped to the hotel where they'd spent last night.

"What do you need?" she asked, pushing the U-lock and dead bolt into place.

"I'm good." He eased himself onto the bed and smiled at her. "Just relax."

"How? You were attacked—"

He wanted to tell her the attack was sloppy, to point out—again—that he'd survived. She needed to hear something else. He understood. "Now you know how I felt last night."

Her mouth closed and her eyes went wide, her dark eyebrows arching, and then she scowled. "Yeah, okay."

She dropped into the chair across the room and he stifled a smirk. "How was the cake tasting?"

"Cake is the least of our concerns," she replied.

He eyed the ring on her finger, liking the look of it there. "They didn't send any samples with you?" That earned him a sharp glare. A smarter man wouldn't bait this particular woman, but he happened to be fond of the way her eyes sparked when she was annoyed.

Fond. Yeah, that was an understatement. Despite the close call, it didn't feel like the right time to tell her how "fond" he was.

"We left in a rush." She stood up and pushed her hands through her hair. "Are you sore? Do you need something for pain?"

"No," he answered. "I only need one thing."

"Tell me," she said, eager to help.

"Come here and kiss me." He hoped it would distract them both from the inevitable talk about the case. When she learned that he'd sent his latest findings and theories to Victoria without consulting her, Frankie would be angry. At the very least.

Before he faced that, he wanted some tangible reassurance they were both still breathing, and committed to this case. To each other. He shoved the errant thought aside. Yes, he needed her touch more than he wanted to admit, but he'd just been shot. Sappy, random things were supposed to wander through his concussed brain.

She walked over, pulled a chair close to the bed and took his hand between hers. "You scared me."

Her quiet admission surprised him. "Given a choice, I'd never do that." He tugged on her hand until she was in range of his lips. For a long moment, he savored the sweet, soft kiss.

Her mouth curved in a gentle smile when she broke away. Then she caught her plump lower lip between her teeth. Stepping out of his reach, she hooked her thumbs into the back pockets of her khaki slacks. "I did something stupid while you were back there," she said. "Before they let me see you."

"How stupid?"

"I lost it." She fixed her gaze on the ceiling and blinked a few times. Her eyes were clear when she focused on him again. "I was scared and mad and confused. I started tossing around accusations about..." She waved a hand in the general direction of his injuries.

"Sophia didn't do this," he blurted.

Frankie dropped her head into her hands, embarrassed. "I blamed Paul, actually."

*"What?"*

"That's not the worst of it."

Aidan waited, impatience and worry clawing at him.

"I nearly blew our cover. I was just so mad. It's one thing to take a shot at me, but you're just along for the ride." Her hands raked through her hair again and she scooped it up on top of her head before letting it fall. "Whether it's Paul, Sophia or both of them behind this, I think I've wrecked the case."

"Frankie—"

She barreled on, "I'm going to confront Mom in the morning." Standing, Frankie paced back and forth along the foot of the bed. "I'll show her what I've found and be satisfied with whatever she does or doesn't say. Then I'll send everything to Victoria for a final decision about notifying any authorities."

"What did you find?" Aidan willed her to

stop pacing and look at him. It was hard enough to concentrate right now without the distraction of her tantalizing body and cascading hair. "Frankie."

She stopped short. "I found travel documents buried in the corporate organization files. They show Mom and Paul returning from Europe the day my unit was attacked. The statement filed in my father's treason case listed her in DC on those days."

"Where were the documents?"

"Archived on the main server."

"You know that can be faked."

She nodded. "Her trips to see me in Bethesda and Atlanta were there, too. I couldn't see any difference. I copied everything for you to review."

"Thanks," he said, watching her place the drive on the table as if it might explode at any second. "I found something today, too."

"Tell me. I have to know, Aidan."

Hearing the pain in her voice, he cleared his throat, wishing he'd had a better choice. "I found Lennox's trail and a charter flight record signed with Sophia's signature stamp. I'd planned to work on it more tonight."

"That's it. I'm going over there right now."

He shook his head, dreading what he needed to say. "No." How did he tell her it was too late? "You can't confront Sophia tonight or to-morrow. I sent everything we've gathered to Victoria. She'll take it to the right people for confirmation."

"You did *what*?"

He watched shock and hurt twist Frankie's beautiful features. He knew she felt betrayed, and with good reason. When he'd walked her through his investigation early this morning, he promised to share everything with her first. "I'm sorry. I was still in the car and I didn't want to take a chance that Paul would finish me off before I reached the hospital."

"Paul?"

Aidan nodded. "I'm sure that's really why he invited me to dinner tonight. My investigation was getting too close. He had to act."

She was on her feet again. "Were they working together? Why did they need to get my dad out of the way?"

"I don't have those answers yet. Victoria—"

Frankie spun around, her long hair fanning out and then settling over her shoulders as the anger returned in a rush. "This was *my* fight, Aidan. Sophia won't ever be honest with me now."

Aidan felt as if he'd taken a punch to the gut. He'd blown it. Not with the case; he'd done the right thing as an investigator. When she calmed down, maybe by the turn of the next century, Frankie would see that, too.

But he'd done it the wrong way for her. Frankie's quest might have looked like vengeance days ago, but he knew better now. He knew *her* better. Frankie was a woman trying to reconcile inconceivable events for the brokenhearted little girl she kept locked away inside. Her father had been her hero. The charges, verdict and suicide were irrelevant. Her mother had been her anchor, the one constant in her life.

Hell, logic and justice were irrelevant at this point. She just wanted to hear the whole story, to understand, if that was possible. She'd never be satisfied, never move forward until she had the truth. And now she'd never trust him enough to give him a chance to share that life.

"I—I'm going out," she said, starting for the door.

Aidan pushed himself to his feet and the room did a slow spin. "Frankie, wait." He couldn't let her leave. Not upset, not alone.

She shook her head. "I can't stay here with you," she said over her shoulder. "I can't trust you."

The words slid through him like one of her lethal knives. The bullet hadn't caused him this much pain. "It's too dangerous. You're a target,"

They just couldn't be sure about the method of the next attack.

Her shoulders rolled back, her spine ramrod straight. "I can take care of myself, Mr. Abbot. You should ask Victoria to check in on you per the concussion protocol."

He swore as Frankie left the room, the door closing with a heavy clack. He wanted to follow her, but with him in this condition she'd easily outpace him. Damned concussion. He wouldn't leave her safety to chance, not after all that had happened. There had to be something he could do, someone he could call to keep an eye on her. Who could he trust?

He stared helplessly at his cell phone. He trusted Frankie. She was the only person in the city he felt he could count on. No one else was worth the risk. Aidan swore again and called her number, praying she'd pick up.

Naturally she didn't. The woman had a temper and this time he couldn't blame her. He'd promised to bring everything to her first and he'd meant to. But he'd mentally applied a caveat that he would bypass her if it kept her out of harm's way.

"How's that working out for you, Abbot?" The answering silence felt like judge and jury.

Aidan used the app on his cell phone to verify that the GPS on her cell was active and working.

When the location came back that she hadn't left the hotel, he breathed a sigh of relief. Assuming she hadn't tossed the device into the trash on her way out the door.

He'd screwed this up beyond all recognition. He could make it right. Ignoring the headache and vertigo, he booted up his laptop and grabbed her flash drive.

She wanted answers? He'd find them, to hell with caution. He did a quick calculation of the time difference as he sorted through the files. One by one, he sent her findings on Sophia and his research of Paul on to an old friend at Interpol. With any luck, an objective opinion would shed some light on what he and Frankie were too close to see.

Whether she could forgive him or not for breaking her trust was another question entirely. Aidan sighed. That answer would have to come later and most likely after much groveling.

He smiled. If it worked, if he won her trust, it would all be worth it.

# *Chapter Thirteen*

Frankie knew Aidan had done the right thing. Though she hated giving in to his safety warning, she went only as far as the hotel bar. She nursed her beer, trying to sort out this ridiculous mess. In his place, targeted by a sniper and sitting next to a potential enemy, she would've done the same thing. Understanding his choice wasn't the same as approving it. Who was she kidding? Holding a grudge against her only ally wouldn't help her unveil the truth.

Ally. What a crock. He'd become far more important than that. Shutting Aidan down only made her stubborn. She ordered a second beer while she figured out her next step with the man and the situation.

She signed the bar tab at the last possible moment and trudged back upstairs. It wasn't safe to leave him alone, no matter how mild the concussion. He was asleep when she walked in, but she could tell he'd tried to work, because his computer was still on and open. She walked over and shook his shoulder, asking him a few standard questions about the day, his name and hers. Satisfied with the answers, she let him drift off to sleep once more.

What a difference twenty-four hours could make. After she was attacked they'd wound up in that bed. Hot. Naked. Together. Her pulse leaped into overdrive at the recollection.

It had been more than wonderful how he'd held her, scars and all. She would savor the memory once they finished here and went their separate ways. Taking a pillow and the extra blanket from the closet, she curled into the lumpy chair to get some rest.

*Thursday, April 14, 6:00 a.m.*

SHE WOKE TO the sound of her cell phone buzzing near her pillow. It was too early for an alarm, but she was wide-awake when she saw the text message. Her mother wanted her to come to the house, alone, to clear the air. This wasn't a talk for the office. Sophia had definitely figured out the happily engaged, prodigal daughter routine was an act.

*Answers at last.* Rolling to her back, Frankie sent a quick affirmative reply.

Last night Aidan's decision about the case had felt like a kick in the teeth. Now it might just be her ace in the hole. It was small comfort that if she and Aidan did wind up dead, the Colby Agency could pursue their killer.

Quietly, she showered and dressed, simultaneously pleased and worried that Aidan slept through it. She roused him just enough for the concussion protocol before leaving him a note about the message from her mother. If Sophia was ready to talk about Frank Leone's downfall, Frankie certainly wasn't going to ignore the summons.

She took the rental car and drove out to Queen Anne, enjoying the lack of traffic at this early hour. She parked at the curb and gave herself a moment to breathe. Which Sophia would be waiting for her, the mother who was eager to salvage a relationship or the professional analyst with layer upon layer of secrets? That was the crux; Frankie didn't know which mom to trust, only which mom she *wanted* to believe.

The front door opened and her mother hovered in the doorway, the smile on her face loaded with tension. Like mother, like daughter, Frankie thought, climbing out of the car. She ignored the catch in her back as she mounted the steps, taking her time so she wouldn't reveal any weakness.

As Frankie reached the porch, Sophia moved as if to hug her, then jerked back. Apparently she didn't know which woman to be in the moment any more than Frankie did. "I made tea," Sophia said, inviting her inside.

The door closed with a bang and Frankie spun around in time to see Paul throwing the lock. "What are *you* doing here?"

"Think of me as a mediator," he said.

Something in his smooth voice made Frankie's skin crawl. "This conversation doesn't concern you." She shot a look at her mother, but Sophia only gave a small shake of her head and a look that told her not to argue. But the days of her blindly obeying her mom were long gone. "What the hell is going on?"

"It does concern me," Paul said, giving her a shove into the kitchen. "You wanted answers, Frankie. I have them." He pulled a gun from his back and a silencer from his pocket, slowly mating the two pieces. "Not that you'll get much time to enjoy the truth."

"You said you loved me." Sophia stared him down, her voice hard as steel. "Prove it. Let her go."

"I loved you once." Paul shoved Frankie into a kitchen chair. "You told me you were giving Frankie space and the next thing I know she winds up in the heart of the company," he countered, his voice rising before he regained control. "With full access. You pushed me into this corner. Now I'm cashing out."

"I don't care about the company," Frankie said, trying to distract him, to get him away from her mom.

"No one does," he announced. "Not like I do."

"Paul, think about what you're doing," Sophia pleaded.

His gaze shifted from Sophia to Frankie and back. "I've thought it all through. I've exhausted the options. We'll have a tidy double homicide, capped with a suicide."

A cold shiver raced down Frankie's back. The hardware in her spine made it worse, driving that chill into her bones. "Leave Aidan out of it." She couldn't bear to know her case had killed him.

"You are clever," Paul said with obvious approval. "But you're weak." He tapped Sophia's shoulder with the silencer. "When I realized you wouldn't see things my way, I knew it was time to make my move."

"See what your way?" Sophia's voice was quiet, urgent. "We're partners! What are you doing?"

"You've blocked me at every turn, darling. It's time for the overseas expansion—"

"The company isn't ready for that," Sophia interrupted.

Paul gestured with the gun and rolled his eyes. "See what I'm up against? The point is, Frankie, I had to do something after she met with Legal and changed the ownership so you had a say in whatever moves we made as a company."

"You did that?" Frankie couldn't believe it. "When were you going to tell me?"

"When I was sure you wouldn't consider it an emotional bribe," Sophia admitted.

A few more pieces clicked into place. She glanced at Paul. "You couldn't kill her until she changed the legalities back in your favor."

"Or unless you die, too."

"You used her," Sophia said through gritted teeth. "You bastard."

Frankie gasped, horrified that his plan had nearly worked.

Paul shrugged. "A man's entitled to hope for an easy road once in a while."

Frankie's stomach twisted. As Aidan and Victoria had feared, she'd been played, from the moment Lennox showed up in Savannah. "You tampered with her statement. Made sure I saw it. The false passports, the safe-deposit box. Everything was a setup to prod a move out of me."

Paul stepped close to her, his eyes sharp and

mean. "You wanted to believe the worst of your mother, a woman who's done nothing but agonize over your distance. It was easy enough to get you out here, wasn't it?" He paced away, turning back before Frankie could make a move. "You idolized your father. It was so easy. You latched on to the 'evidence' against her like a dog with a bone."

An ugly image, but she couldn't argue with the truth of it. "You sent me on a wild-goose chase."

"So predictable," he said with a sneer. "I had to do something when I caught her watching your career in Savannah."

"Of course I watched her career," Sophia snapped, tears spilling down her cheeks. "She's my *daughter.*"

Paul shook his head. "Women are soft. Shortsighted. Family and sentiment have no place in business. Trust me, Sophia, I will take good care of Leo Solutions."

Sophia swore at him. "It was never *your* dream."

Frankie looked at her mother and didn't see anything that resembled soft right now. Her face was set with a grim determination, and Frankie knew she was looking for a way to get them out of this.

"You set up my dad," she guessed, trying to

keep Paul talking while she racked her brain for the right maneuver. "You insinuated yourself into a place that should've been his."

"He got himself into that mess. I just made sure the pieces fell where I could pick them up." Paul gave a sharp bark of bitter laughter. "You should've been mine all along." He sneered at Sophia. "Frank stole you from me. I waited a very long time to take him out of the picture and reclaim what belonged to me."

Sophia's eyes went wide. "You blew that operation and pinned it on Frank?" She leaped forward and slapped Paul across the cheek, leaving a red handprint behind. "Innocent people died that day."

Frankie felt equally blindsided. She'd misinterpreted everything. Her mother hadn't been any more informed about her father's treason than anyone else. Her sworn statement had been little more than a report. Paul had been the one who'd painted the gray area and ruined the Leones and the lives of countless others in the process.

He gripped Sophia's arm and shoved her hard into the counter. Frankie jumped up, but Paul leveled the gun at her mother's forehead. "You ready to say goodbye?"

"No!" Frankie held up her hands and sat down again, ruthlessly ignoring the catch in her hip.

"You don't have to do this, Paul. Dad's gone. Walk away now."

"You won't let me go that easy."

"Let us live and I'll forget you ever existed," Frankie promised.

"I know better. I've watched you." Paul glowered at her. "You should've died, but you're as stubborn as your father. I'm not leaving anything more to chance. Consider this a hostile takeover."

Sophia stood there, silent, unmoving, Paul's hand ruthlessly gripping her arm. Frankie recognized her intention. Her husband had been framed and murdered, her family destroyed, and Sophia was calculating how to save her daughter. Frankie sent a silent plea with her eyes for her mom to be patient. She refused to lose her to this madman the way she'd lost her dad.

"Don't do it," Frankie screamed, though her mother hadn't moved a muscle.

Startled, Paul whipped around, leading with his gun. Frankie lunged, going for his knees. The weapon fired with a muffled pop and she could only pray the bullet had missed her mom.

The gun clattered across the tile and Frankie grappled with Paul, trying to keep him down. Her navy training kept her in the fight, but he was bigger, with a longer reach. He punched her and rolled away. She pulled her knife from the sheath at her waist and put herself between him and the gun, between him and her mother.

He lunged, she ducked under his defenses, her blade slicing through his shirt, and a thin line of blood followed. She heard her mother calling the police. All she had to do was keep him here, keep him busy, and it would all be over.

Sophia threw herself at him. Somewhere across the room Frankie could hear the 9-1-1 operator asking the nature of the emergency. Paul punched Sophia in the face. When she hit the floor, he grabbed her by the hair and pounded her head against the hardwood.

"Mom!" Frankie rushed toward him.

AIDAN HEARD THE noisy fight as he broke through the back door and into the kitchen, gun drawn. Sophia was on the floor. Not moving. Frankie was fighting Paul. Aidan lined up a shot, but they flipped and he couldn't take it without risking hitting her. Sweat poured down his face. His body shook with the effort of staying vertical.

He shouted a warning, but Paul didn't heed it. He plowed a fist into Frankie's stomach, followed by a shoulder, driving her back into the wall. Aidan rushed forward and the room spun. Damn it! His vision cleared just in time for him to see Frankie trying to get up and Paul smirking down at her,

"Move away from her," Aidan shouted. "Or I will blow your damn head off."

"Whatever you say." Paul raised his hands as if in surrender, but then twisted and kicked Frankie in the back.

Aidan fired twice, putting the first bullet in Paul's knee, the second in his shoulder. The coward howled in pain. "Stay down or the next one will be between your eyes."

Aidan rushed to Frankie and fell to his knees beside her. Almost too terrified to touch her, he took stock. She was breathing, blood smearing her nose and lip. Paul had given her hell in the brief fight, but she'd held her own.

"Frankie," he said. She didn't respond. The vicious bastard had executed that last kick where he knew it would do the most damage. Aidan had no idea if it was safe to touch her or to move her. He wouldn't take any chances. "Talk to me. Come on. Please, Francesca."

He smoothed her hair back from her face. He'd called for help en route. Where the hell were the authorities? If he'd only moved faster…

"Frankie?" Sophia was up on her hands and knees, crawling toward them. "Oh, my God." A keening sound issued from her throat.

Aidan handed her his weapon. "Make sure he stays put until the authorities arrive."

Sophia, her face swollen and battered, accepted the weapon and turned it on her lover. "Devil," she spat.

"Come on, Frankie." Aidan clutched her limp hand between his, raising it to his lips. She had to wake up. She had to survive so he could beg her forgiveness and tell her he loved her. He couldn't accept any other outcome.

"She's strong," Sophia said quietly. "Strong and stubborn."

"He kicked her in the back," Aidan said, his voice cracking with fear. This couldn't be happening again.

"You'll see," Sophia promised. "She'll be fine." A sob choked out of her. "She has to be."

Aidan wasn't convinced. There was a bruise blooming on her cheek, a thin line of blood just showing in her hairline. "I'll kill him," he whispered. He aimed a look at the worthless coward now curled in the fetal position. "For every scratch, I'll—"

"Aidan?"

Frankie's thin voice yanked him away from his dark thoughts. "I'm right here." He squeezed her hand.

"How?" She tried to look around, grimaced for her trouble. "When…did you get here?"

"Not soon enough," he said. Sirens sounded in the distance. "Help is almost here."

The police arrived, bringing a new onslaught

of chaos. Paul was arrested and taken away, while paramedics rushed in to tend to the injured.

"I'm okay," Frankie insisted. She tried to push herself upright, but Aidan stopped her.

"Let the paramedics do their job," he ordered.

Relieved of holding the gun on Paul, Sophia moved closer to her daughter. "Where does it hurt, honey?"

"Everywhere," Frankie admitted.

"Thank God," Aidan breathed. He'd been worried Paul's malicious attack might have paralyzed her again. Frankie was strong, but he'd do anything to spare her another debilitating injury and arduous recovery. "You're still going to the hospital."

She tried to shake her head. "I don't need to go."

"Just a precaution," Sophia added as paramedics treated her. "Don't argue with your mother."

"But I do it so well," Frankie said, her lips twitching into a lopsided grin.

Her hand still in his, Aidan kissed her. "Play nice," he reminded her, much as he'd done their first day here.

"Yes, dear," she replied in kind.

He stayed by her side, releasing her hand only when ordered to do so by the paramedic team.

He rode with her in the ambulance and walked beside her until they wheeled her away for testing at the hospital.

Over two hours later, Sophia found him in the waiting area and he accepted the coffee she'd brought along. "Any word?"

"Not yet."

"She's a fighter."

"I'm aware," he said.

"She's lucky to have a fiancé like you."

"I'm the lucky one." He studied his coffee, certain that if he looked Sophia in the eye, she'd see his guilt over lying to her about their engagement. Would it take the sting out of the deception if he told her he loved Frankie and planned to convince her to marry him?

"She loves you, too, you know," Sophia said.

Aidan kept his mouth shut. Any reply would only make things worse.

"I think it's best if we reschedule the wedding for the spring. It will give your family more time to adjust to the news."

Now Aidan looked up. "My family?" The Colby Agency should've intercepted any inquiries about his real family to maintain the cover.

"I may be a romantic," Sophia admitted with a shy smile, "but I'm not a complete idiot. Not about my daughter, anyway."

Aidan leaned back in the waiting room chair, laughing. "You knew from the beginning."

"I knew she wanted me to believe it," Sophia said. "And I might confess to making extravagant plans in an effort to break her. You're not going to let her off the hook, are you?"

"I love her," Aidan said. "And I like the look of that diamond ring on her finger."

"You have excellent taste. In women and jewelry." Sophia stood, urging him up as well so she could give him a real hug. "Welcome to the family."

"That might be premature. It could take some time to sell your daughter on that whole love, marriage and commitment idea."

"Do you like chocolate cake?"

"It's my favorite."

Sophia nodded as if that answered everything. "Have faith. My daughter's a smart girl. She'll come around."

He hoped she was right. "The Leone women are a tough breed."

"Don't you ever forget it, young man."

Aidan thought his future mother-in-law, though a little daunting, would be an asset. He checked the clock on the wall, hoping it wouldn't be much longer before he could see the woman who'd captured his heart. While they waited, he and Sophia tossed around real wedding plans, just in case Frankie agreed to stick with him.

Medical staff came and went, and Aidan's patience was gone by the time the doors parted and Frankie appeared.

She walked toward him carefully, her face pale and her smile wide. It took him a minute to process that it was her, upright and steady. Leaping to his feet, he hurried forward, wrapping his arms around her and breathing her in. "You're okay? You're really okay?"

Her cheek rubbed against his chest as she nodded. "Told you I wouldn't break." She hugged him gingerly, mindful of his stitches. "Thanks for saving the day."

"Anytime. Every time. You can trust me." He dropped to one knee, holding her left hand in his.

"What are you doing?" Her big brown eyes were round with surprise.

He felt people staring at them and didn't give a damn. "I won't waste one more second. I love you, Francesca Leone. Marry me."

"Oh, Aidan." She covered her lips with her free hand. "I—"

"Say yes." He cut her off, terrified she wouldn't say what he needed to hear. Gently, his thumb stroked her finger just above the ring. "Please, say yes, make me the happiest man on the planet. Say yes, for real this time. Forever."

He heard a sniffle and knew Sophia's heart was on her sleeve. But Frankie continued staring at him with an unreadable expression. What was going on behind those stunning eyes?

"Aidan." She pulled him to his feet and kissed him as tears slid down her cheeks. "Yes," she whispered against his lips. "You're more than I deserve." She stopped his protest with another soft kiss. "I love you, too. For real. Forever."

# *Chapter Fourteen*

*Chicago,*
*Friday, April 15, 6:30 a.m.*

Victoria sipped her coffee and hummed in satisfaction. "Lucas, this coffee is amazing. Is it something new?"

Her handsome husband winked at her. "I selected various beans and ground it myself."

Victoria smiled. "Well, it's wonderful."

"Thank you, my dear."

She thought of her friend Sophia and all she had suffered with the devastation leading up to her husband's death last year. Not to mention all those months of being estranged from her daughter. The mystery shrouding that terrible time remained unsolved. Aidan and Frankie had uncovered the evil that had kept mother and daughter apart, but the rest...there were still few answers

"You're worried about Sophia," Lucas guessed.

He could always read her so well. "She's flying to Chicago on Monday. We're having dinner. I told her you'd be joining us."

"Of course. Is this about what happened to the general?"

"She says she has a business appointment, but I'm hoping she'll allow the Colby Agency to help her find the truth."

Lucas nodded. "If anyone can find it, the agency can."

"I'm certain we'll hear all about Aidan and Frankie's wedding plans."

Lucas reached across the table and squeezed his wife's hand. "There's nothing like a wedding celebration to remind us all how special true love is."

Victoria was lucky to have found true love twice in her life. She hoped Sophia Leone would be as fortunate.

Only time would tell.

\* \* \* \* \*

*Look for Sophia's story
coming next month in
HEAVY ARTILLERY HUSBAND!*

# LARGER-PRINT BOOKS!

**HARLEQUIN**

*Presents*®

## GET 2 FREE LARGER-PRINT NOVELS PLUS 2 FREE GIFTS!

PASSION GUARANTEED SEDUCTION

**YES!** Please send me 2 FREE LARGER-PRINT Harlequin Presents® novels and my 2 FREE gifts (gifts are worth about $10). After receiving them, if I don't wish to receive any more books, I can return the shipping statement marked "cancel." If I don't cancel, I will receive 6 brand-new novels every month and be billed just $5.30 per book in the U.S. or $5.74 per book in Canada. That's a saving of at least 12% off the cover price! It's quite a bargain! Shipping and handling is just 50¢ per book in the U.S. and 75¢ per book in Canada.* I understand that accepting the 2 free books and gifts places me under no obligation to buy anything. I can always return a shipment and cancel at any time. Even if I never buy another book, the two free books and gifts are mine to keep forever.

176/376 HDN GHVY

| | |
|---|---|
| Name | (PLEASE PRINT) |

| | |
|---|---|
| Address | Apt. # |

| | | |
|---|---|---|
| City | State/Prov. | Zip/Postal Code |

Signature (if under 18, a parent or guardian must sign)

### Mail to the **Reader Service:**
**IN U.S.A.:** P.O. Box 1867, Buffalo, NY 14240-1867
**IN CANADA:** P.O. Box 609, Fort Erie, Ontario L2A 5X3

**Are you a subscriber to Harlequin Presents® books
and want to receive the larger-print edition?
Call 1-800-873-8635 today or visit us at www.ReaderService.com.**

\* Terms and prices subject to change without notice. Prices do not include applicable taxes. Sales tax applicable in N.Y. Canadian residents will be charged applicable taxes. Offer not valid in Quebec. This offer is limited to one order per household. Not valid for current subscribers to Harlequin Presents Larger-Print books. All orders subject to credit approval. Credit or debit balances in a customer's account(s) may be offset by any other outstanding balance owed by or to the customer. Please allow 4 to 6 weeks for delivery. Offer available while quantities last.

**Your Privacy**—The Reader Service is committed to protecting your privacy. Our Privacy Policy is available online at www.ReaderService.com or upon request from the Reader Service.

We make a portion of our mailing list available to reputable third parties that offer products we believe may interest you. If you prefer that we not exchange your name with third parties, or if you wish to clarify or modify your communication preferences, please visit us at www.ReaderService.com/consumerchoice or write to us at Reader Service Preference Service, P.O. Box 9062, Buffalo, NY 14240-9062. Include your complete name and address.

HPLP15

# LARGER-PRINT BOOKS!
## GET 2 FREE LARGER-PRINT NOVELS PLUS
## 2 FREE GIFTS!

**HARLEQUIN®**

*super romance®*

## More Story...More Romance

HSRLP15

**YES!** Please send me **The Montana Mavericks Collection** in Larger Print. This collection begins with **3 FREE** books and **2 FREE** gifts (gifts valued at approx. $20.00 retail) in the first shipment, along with the other first 4 books from the collection! If I do not cancel, I will receive 8 monthly shipments until I have the entire 51-book Montana Mavericks collection. I will receive 2 or 3 FREE books in each shipment and I will pay just $4.99 US/ $5.89 CDN for each of the other four books in each shipment, plus $2.99 for shipping and handling per shipment.*If I decide to keep the entire collection, I'll have paid for only 32 books, because 19 books are FREE! I understand that accepting the 3 free books and gifts places me under no obligation to buy anything. I can always return a shipment and cancel at any time. My free books and gifts are mine to keep no matter what I decide.

263 HCN 2404   463 HCN 2404

Name _____ (PLEASE PRINT) _____

Address _____ Apt. # _____

City _____ State/Prov. _____ Zip/Postal Code _____

Signature (if under 18, a parent or guardian must sign) _____

### Mail to the **Reader Service:**
**IN U.S.A.:** P.O. Box 1867, Buffalo, NY 14240-1867
**IN CANADA:** P.O. Box 609, Fort Erie, Ontario L2A 5X3